ESCAPE THE ROOM

STEPHEN MANGAN

ILLUSTRATED BY ANITA MANGAN

D0263031

WITHDRAWN FROM STOCK

For Mum and Dad

Don't look down, Jack told himself, *just don't look down.*

The man, Jack had already forgotten his name, unbolted the gate and swung it open. He fixed it in place. There was now nothing between Jack and the drop. The woman, who Jack thought was called Tilly, gave him an encouraging smile.

Why had he agreed to this? Even now, he wasn't sure.

He placed his hands on the railing and shuffled his feet forward until his toes poked over the edge. He glanced down and immediately wished he hadn't.

Far, far below him was the fair: the carousel, the little roller coaster, the Waltzer.

The cage swayed in the breeze. It was quiet up here. Odd sounds drifted up, people screaming on the Pirate Ship, a mishmash of music, a siren in the distance. Above them, the cables attaching the cage to the crane creaked and groaned.

The long elastic rope hung beneath.

Jack looked for his dad. He wasn't hard to spot. The only person standing still in a stream of fairgoers, poring over his phone, flicking through the photos of Jack he'd taken minutes earlier, oblivious to the inconvenience he was causing.

He'd have a heart attack if he knew I was up here, thought Jack.

Jack glanced behind him. The man and Tilly gave him a nod. He took a deep breath. As he had been instructed, he lifted his arms straight in front of him and leaned forward.

His throat was dry. He felt sweat prickle all over his body.

I could still stop this, he thought. He hadn't yet got to the point of no return. He could turn around. There was still time to place his hands back on the railing and say to Tilly, "I've changed my mind. I've decided I don't want to throw myself head-first out of a stupidly high cage, suspended from a stupidly big crane, and fall through the air towards the stupidly hard ground. Sorry, I don't know what I was thinking."

He could still have done that. But he didn't.

He leaned forward. His mind was racing but his body moved in slow motion. When you lean forward, he noticed, the first bit happens quite slowly: you're just leaning forward. But it'll get to the point where gravity takes over and the slow lean forward will become a breakneck plunge.

I think I'm past the point where I can stop this, he thought.

Yes, I am definitely past that point now. I'm going to fall.

Without thinking, Jack bent his knees and jumped, throwing his body forward into space, flinging his arms out wide like wings.

From a distance, it looked graceful, majestic, but no one was watching. Now upside down and falling freely, Jack straightened his arms above his head and held his body in a perfect line, an Olympic diver about to enter the water.

He fell, picking up speed at an incredible rate, the wind roaring in his ears, cold and loud. Faster and faster.

This is where the rope tightens, he thought, *this is where the rope stops me falling and I bounce back up again. They just leave it to the last minute to make it extra exciting.*

Right about now. . .

The ground rushed towards him, and it looked like there might be no way he could stop in time. Was this the thrill of it? Was this why people did it? Feeling you were going to hit the ground and then at the last moment – phew! – saved. The rope would tighten, he'd slow to a brief stop and then be thrown into reverse, back up into the sky, and it would all be over.

Any moment now.

Now?

Oh no. . .

Arrow-straight, arms and fingers extended, body vertical, mouth open, Jack hit solid ground at high speed.

And went right through it, with a small,

muffled *plop*.

Like dropping a bowling ball into a vat of jelly.

The ground folded around him and swallowed him up.

There was no trace of any impact, no sign that the earth had been disturbed.

The only clue as to what had happened was the tight, quivering elastic rope coming out of the ground, connected to the cage far above.

That was not how Jack had thought his evening was going to pan out.

Earlier on, Jack and his dad had gone to the funfair, the way they always did on Jack's birthday. Jack hadn't really wanted to, not this year, but his dad had insisted. And during the evening his dad had taken a lot of photos of Jack. Way more than normal. He wasn't good at taking pictures. His technique was to point his phone and click away, hoping that one of them would turn out to be good. The photos Jack's dad had taken in front of the Sky Scream were the final straw.

"You finished, Dad?"

"Just one more. And smile, Jack! Not like that, that looks fake. Smile normally. No, that looks creepy."

Jack had wanted to explain that his smile didn't look real because it wasn't real, but he had said nothing. He often said nothing. It was easier that way.

This particular photo session had been especially embarrassing not just because they were at the funfair, surrounded by crowds of people, but because behind his dad a group of six boys from Jack's school had been queueing at Sizzlers burger van. Jack hoped they wouldn't see him. He used to hang around with these boys and he used to really make them laugh. But lately they had started to avoid him, not inviting him to the park after school or to play at their houses.

Jack couldn't blame them. He wasn't much fun these days.

Fortunately, they were otherwise engaged trying to snatch the hat off the head of the smallest boy, Niblet. Niblet was not enjoying the game at all. They always picked on Niblet.

The stench of frying onions and vinegar coming from Sizzlers was making Jack feel queasy. He risked a glance over to the boys.

Niblet had finally lost his cool and punched Beano in the arm. Beano put Niblet in a headlock. Beano was called Beano because he could inhale a baked bean via his nostril

and often did.

Jack's dad had wanted them to go on the Sky Scream, the scariest ride in the whole fair.

"No way," Jack had said, but his dad wasn't having that and had tried to get Jack to change his mind.

"Oh, come on, Jack, surely you want to try it?"

"I'm good thanks, Dad."

"Oh, Jack-Jack. You don't want me telling everyone you were too scared, do you?"

"I suppose not."

"You'll love it once you're actually on it!"

"Nah, I'm OK."

"Jack, you're annoying me now, just go on the ride!"

"Let's do a different one. . ."

"Come on, J, please."

"Seriously, Dad, I don't want to."

His dad sulked. **"If you don't go on that ride we're going home."**

"That's fine by me."

"Well, that's ridiculous, all the money I've spent on you tonight. You're acting like a child."

Jack had wanted to say, "I *am* a child," but he didn't. Instead, he said something much worse.

"Mum wouldn't make me go on it."

For a moment there was silence.

Jack had brought up his mum. That was the nuclear option. It got him out of the argument, but it was too big a weapon for this fight. A bomb that had taken them both out. They had both lost.

"Let's just take a photo in front of it then, shall we?" Dad said weakly, forcing a smile. Jack had posed for the photo but felt wretched.

Jack didn't want to be at the fair, and Jack

knew his dad didn't want to be there either. They were both trying to please each other but neither of them was happy.

When Mum was alive, it had been a family tradition to visit this fair each year on Jack's birthday. Coming this year was Jack's dad's way of saying things would be all right, things would carry on, that some things hadn't changed. But everything had changed.

The lads from his school had been served their food. Niblet sneaked up behind Beano as he was squirting ketchup on his burger and kicked it out of his hands. The meat, ketchup and onions arced through the air then splattered on to the flattened grass. Niblet sprinted off into the crowd, whooping with delight.

Jack's dad took yet another picture.

Jack had to get out of there.

"Dad, I need the loo," he lied.

Jack rushed off, but almost immediately the slow flow of people he had been impatiently trying to squeeze past had ground to a halt and he was stuck.

He looked back to see if he should give up on this idea and return to his dad, but there were as many people behind him as in front. Jack looked at the ground and sighed. He felt hopeless, again. He should have just gone on the ride so that this whole trip, this misjudged attempt of his father's to have fun, would have been over sooner and then they could have gone home and Jack could hide in his room again. Every decision he made at the moment seemed to be the wrong one.

Jack pushed his way through the mass of

people, hemmed in by dozens of anoraks and overcoats.

Just then, the crowd parted and Jack could see clearly. And there, in a gap between the fairground stalls, was a woman. She was watching him.

It was ... his mum.

Jack froze; time slowed.

For one heartbeat the world stopped.

Jack stood and looked, unable to process what he was seeing.

The crowd surged forward, blocking Jack's view once more, and the world flooded back in – sound, breath and sensation.

No, was his first thought. *No. That's not her. It can't be her. She's dead.*

When the crowd parted again, she was gone. No woman, no mum, no one there. Had he imagined it? He had to find out. Jack headed towards the spot where he had seen her, a narrow passage between the fairground stalls that led towards a patch of woodland, and walked down it. Picking his way carefully across the thick electrical cables underfoot, he edged into the darkness.

Behind him the hustle and bustle of the fair faded away. He almost lost his balance in the gloom and, as he went to steady himself, was surprised by the loud *clang* his hand made as it slammed into the metal wall.

Emerging into a patch of open ground, his eyes took a moment to adjust to the darkness. The temperature felt noticeably cooler back here and the breeze smelled of wet grass and petrol.

There she was, walking away from him.

He went to call out, but no words came. He stumbled towards her, and just then she turned.

It wasn't her.

Of course, he thought, of course it wasn't. How could it have been? He felt foolish and embarrassed.

There was a bit of a resemblance, the same colour hair, about the same height but … it wasn't her.

"Do you want to do a bungee jump?" the woman asked.

Jack half-smiled and shook his head. "No way."

Behind the woman, in a metal cage that came up to his waist, stood a man holding a sign that read:

The cage was attached to an enormous crane.

"We're really not supposed to be here," said

the woman. "Can you keep a secret?"

The man and the woman smiled at Jack.

I should leave, Jack thought.

"I don't like heights," he said. "I'm going now."

But he didn't.

"I'm not doing a bungee jump," he said, walking over to the cage as though pushed by invisible hands. "I watched my dad do one once. It took him ages to jump. He said you can't believe how high up you are, and your body and mind are screaming, **'DANGER!!'** and every fibre of your being is telling you not to do it. So, yeah, it's not really for me, free or not."

He stepped into the cage through the little metal gate held open for him by the man.

"I'm Tilly, that's Bobby," the woman said. "Do you want to do a bungee jump? You don't have to."

"No. I don't. Absolutely not!" Jack laughed and Tilly laughed too.

They stood, smiling at each other.

Then Jack found himself saying this:

"Well, I suppose I could do one. Why not?"

For the briefest fraction of a second, as the ground hurtled towards him, faster than his mind could process, he knew he was in huge trouble. But then the earth and the blackness folded in around him and he lost all sensation.

He became aware that he'd stopped falling.

He felt no pain.

He was hanging, upside down, in the dark.

With a jolt, he realized he wasn't alone. Close by, lying with her arms outstretched, was a girl.

She was about the same age as him.
They looked at one another.

She's under the ground, Jack thought, *and so am I.*

Jack became aware that someone was screaming hysterically and he wished they would stop.

Then he realized that the person screaming hysterically was him.

The girl stared.

It was understandable that he was howling uncontrollably, he thought.

He had been about to die, smashed to mush on the ground, but he was fairly sure he was still alive.

He *must* be alive. He didn't think he'd be able to scream like this if he were dead.

Yes, this was happening: he was hanging upside down, underground maybe, with a girl close by, and he was wailing.

Then Jack noticed he was screaming a little less.

He stopped screaming.

He looked around him. It was too dark to see much, but he couldn't make out any walls or even a floor. It was hot, dark and humid. A cave, maybe.

The girl spoke.

"What are you looking at?" she said.

Jack tried to shrug but he discovered it's

quite hard to shrug when you are upside down dangling from a rope. His mouth was open; his eyes were wild; he looked like he'd seen a ghost.

Before Jack could speak there was a creaking sound from above and he felt the harness start to slide open. His legs were released, and he fell, again, but this time on to hard ground. He flung his arms out to break his fall, giving his elbow an almighty crack.

And then the lights came on.

The lights were ridiculously bright. They both shut their eyes, momentarily blinded. They lifted their hands in front of their faces as if that was going to help. Which it wasn't.

They tried to open their eyes, but you can't rush these things. Eyes need a certain amount of time to sort themselves out. Eyes have a mind of their own and they won't open until they think it's safe to do so.

Although their ears were working hard to make up for the lack of information from their eyes, they weren't having much luck either. It was pretty silent.

"What's your name?" the girl whispered.

"Me?" asked Jack.

"Yes, of course you. Who else would I be talking to?"

"I don't know," Jack snapped back. This had been a challenging few minutes in his life.

Plus, his arm hurt.

"Jack," he said tersely. **"My name is Jack."**

"I'm Cally," she said. "It looks like we're in this together, so be cool and don't get your big-boy pants in a twist."

Jack was about to ask her what exactly they were in together: how did she know that they were in something together? What did she mean, exactly, by big-boy pants? And why should he have to keep them untwisted, because, after all, he'd just fallen out of a crane and through the ground into a dark (now light) cave that may or may not be a cave and he had landed upside down next to a total stranger who was now being a tiny bit RUDE? All these thoughts were about to form into a sentence when they heard a door unlock in the distance.

They opened their eyes.

The place was big. So big that they couldn't see the end of it, the edges of it. No walls, no ceiling. Just bright whiteness stretching in all directions. Vast.

They were standing on something that, at least, they could see and feel – a flat, white, smooth floor.

Jack realized he was so rigid with tension that he was holding his breath. He let it out again, feeling a little light-headed.

Cally looked at Jack and said in a small, quiet voice, "Are we dead?"

Jack's heart dropped into his feet. Dead? Could they be? Certainly, this might be some sort of heaven – blinding white light in all directions. Perhaps that *is* what had happened to him. He'd hit the ground and not gone through it at all but died there and then and here he was ... in heaven. The thought plummeted through the centre of his being like hot sauce through whipped cream. He was in heaven with a girl who was making comments about him wearing big-boy pants.

"Why did you have a rope tied to your feet?" asked Cally.

"I was doing a bungee jump."

"Why?"

"I don't know, I just did one. I don't know what's going on."

They were interrupted by the sound of a woman singing.

"Doo-be-doo!! Doo-be-doo-be-DOO! Be-doo-be-doo-be-doo-doo. Oh I wanna wanna wanna and you wanna wanna wanna. In fact, we both wanna wanna wanna..."

There was a pause. Then at the top of her voice, *"DON'T WEEEEEEEEEEEEEEEE?"* Her voice was warm and husky but she wasn't a good singer. She was an actively bad singer, and her singing sounded like she was going to do herself an injury, but she seemed to be enjoying herself immensely.

"Yes! Oh yes! Oh yes yes yes! Hold me

close. Hold me face. Hold me coat. Hold me bag it's HEEEEEAAAA.......VY..."

And out of the whiteness, she appeared. She was incredibly skinny, incredibly tall, maybe twice the height of Jack, with large red lips and plenty of teeth. Too many teeth. She looked like she was breaking a set of teeth in for someone else. There was a large gap between the front two that you could easily fit a pound coin through. Horizontally. She had shoulder-length, jet-black hair. She wore a green dress with a slit in the front that trailed behind her, and her heels click-clacked as she walked towards them.

"Because I have a doo-be-doo-be-doo and you have a doo-be-doo-be-doo-doo," she sang, *"and I be your doo and you doo my be. DON'T WEEEEEEEEEEEEEE?"*

She was smiling as she sang, and every few steps would incorporate a little dance move into her walk.

"When all the doo be done, then don't be doing your doo on my beeeeeeee."

She walked right up to them and, as it became clear that she had no intention of stopping, they jumped apart to let her pass.

"Because I'm telling..." She took a huge

breath and spun around.

**"YOOOOOOOOOOOOOOOOOOOOOOOOO
UUUUUUUUUUUUUUUUUUUUUUUUU–"**

Another big breath.

**"–UUUUUUUUUUUUUUUUUUUUUUUUUUUU
that I'm gonna gonna gonna..."**

She grinned and said, "And that's as far as I've got." She leaned in towards them conspiratorially and murmured huskily, "What d'ya reckon? Did you like it? My song?" She cocked her head to one side and placed a hand behind her ear as if to say "I'm listening".

Jack couldn't speak. The song was so rubbish this had to be some sort of trick.

Maybe she wanted him to say it was good when it was clearly rubbish. Or maybe she thought it was fantastic and didn't know how rubbish it was and just wanted him to say he liked it. Perhaps she really didn't mind what they thought of it, or perhaps this was an incredibly dangerous moment. Why wasn't Cally saying anything? This silence was getting awkward.

"It's brilliant!" he said enthusiastically. **"Absolutely brilliant. I loved it."**

The woman's face lit up. "Really?" she beamed. "You're not just saying that?"

"Oh no, it's wonderful. You sing with panache. You must finish it. What's it called?"

"I don't have a name for it," the woman said. "Yet."

She winked at Jack, who giggled. "Love your dress too," he said. "Beautiful."

"Thank you," the woman purred and, taking a few steps back, flung both her hands into the air, flicked one leg out to the side with the toe of her shoe on the ground and closed her eyes.

She snapped her arms down. **"Good. Moving along then, here we go, let's do this."**

She spun away from them, lowered her head, put both arms out and flicked her fingers to point away from her. A pause. She turned back and said softly and quickly, "Just so you know, I'm starting from the top. This is what you should have had the first time around, but I just wanted to sing my song to you. Couldn't resist. I am not supposed to start like that, I'm supposed to start like this, so imagine this is me starting, that this is the first thing you got from me."

She turned away again and resumed her stance. Then turned again.

"By the way, I'm so pleased you felt I had

panache," she said to Jack. "That's *exactly* what I was going for! Exactly!" She winked at him. "Right, here we go. This time I mean it."

She turned away again and there was a pause. Jack risked a glance at Cally and noticed she looked furious. That little exchange had so enthused both Jack and the woman that they were glowing. It was as if they had each given the other something precious. But the song had been rubbish, thought Jack – he'd really been sort of lying when he had said it was wonderful. He had told the woman what he thought she wanted to hear. He had, as usual, pretended everything was fine. Was that why Cally was angry?

Jack normally felt like he was on the outside of everything, looking in. It took him time to come out of his shell with new people; his dad called him a "slow-burn", and he could often feel himself holding back. Partly because he'd rather not say anything than say something obviously fake. He was always certain they'd see right through it. He was a terrible liar.

So he was thrilled that he'd said the right thing here, but was now anxious in case Cally felt left out.

The woman dropped into a deep curtsey with her head bowed. She rose to her full height, her expression mournful, and looked directly at them.

"WELCOME!" she bellowed. **"WELCOME!"** – then breathily – **"to the Rooms."**

The room – if it was a room, it was hard to tell – began to spin. Or at least that's how it felt to Jack. Slowly at first but speeding up.

"Don't be afraid, Jack and Cally," the woman said, smiling. "Go with it. If you resist you just won't enjoy it as much, I promise you that."

Jack looked over to Cally – how did this woman know their names?

"LOOK AT ME!" she screamed, and they snapped back to her.

The woman looked momentarily furious but then smiled a dazzling smile and continued more calmly. "Sorry to shout but, you know, I've gone to a lot of trouble." She took a deep breath. "Where was I? Oh yes, Jack. And Cally. Let me introduce myself. My name is Wanda. Wanda Full. But you can call me Bertie. I mean, call me Bertie if you like, but that's not my name. My name is Wanda. I just told you. Pay attention. Now. You are probably wondering why you are here. You are probably wondering what's going to happen to you. You might even be hungry and wonder if there's going to be food. And that's good! That's right and that's proper. I'm going to answer the first question." She cleared her throat. "You are here, because you are here. If you weren't here, where would you be? You'd be somewhere else. And that would be wrong."

Jack didn't dare look over to Cally but desperately wanted to know what she was thinking.

Wanda continued: "The Rooms are here for you and you are here for the Rooms. To get to where you need to be, you will have to journey through them. One by one. A room at a time. How do you get out of one room and into the next? Good question, Wanda! Through a door. Sounds simple, right? And to get through each door you'll need a key. How do you get the key? You'll figure it out."

Jack stole a glance at Cally. She still looked

angry but she seemed to be concentrating hard on what Wanda was saying.

Wanda continued: "Find the key in each room and then move on. Room by room until you finish. Got it?"

Wanda didn't wait for an answer. She lowered her voice dramatically and said, "But beware. There are very real dangers. You what?! You heard me, dangers. Don't underestimate them and don't split up. Stick together. Together you'll have the stuff you need. The wherewithal. The ammo. The intellectual and emotional weaponry. *Together.* Got it?"

Wanda nodded her head vigorously.

"Right," she said. "Do you have any questions?"

She shook her head vigorously from side to side and silently mouthed, "Don't ask any questions."

Jack, of course,
had a thousand
questions.

He wanted to know
where he was, what had
happened to him, why he was
there, why the bungee jump
hadn't killed him, who Cally
was, why she was there too, what
this rooms thing meant, how dangerous was it
going to be, and nine-hundred-and-ninety-two
other things, including what time dinner was
and whether there were any snacks because he
suddenly felt ravenously hungry.

"COME ON!" Wanda yelled. **"YOU MUST
HAVE ONE QUESTION!!?!"**

Jack opened his mouth to speak.

"GREAT!" she shouted. **"NO QUESTIONS.**

Come and meet Gary."

Wanda closed her eyes, bent her legs, threw her arms above her head and jumped back and over, executing a beautiful, perfect, elegant backwards dive.

When her fingers reached the ground, they dissolved into it, just melted into it as if she was sliding into an endless pool of white paint.

And she was gone.

Ripples spread out in every direction. Jack and Cally bobbed up and down, as though they were rowing boats riding an ocean swell. Jack cautiously stamped his foot on the ground. It still felt solid.

Jack turned to Cally. She was staring furiously at him, breathing heavily.

"What?" ventured Jack. "Why are you looking at me like that?"

"You better start talking," she hissed, "and make it good."

"Talk about what?"

"ABOUT EVERYTHING!" Cally shouted. "What is happening? Who are you? Why are we here? I've had enough of this crap and I want to go home – is that clear enough for you?"

Her fists were tightly clenched and there were tears in her eyes.

"I don't know," Jack said

honestly. "I don't know any more than you. I went bungee jumping by mistake and now I'm here."

"I don't believe you," Cally replied. "I think this is some cruel joke and it isn't funny any more."

"If this is a joke then I'm not laughing," said Jack.

There was silence while Cally searched his face for clues.

"How did *you* get here?" he asked as gently as he could.

"I'm not going to tell you that," Cally shot back. "I don't have to tell you anything. Who are you?"

Cally was dressed in clothes slightly too big for her, Jack noticed, including a jacket that he'd initially assumed was a school blazer but he could now see wasn't. There was no school badge and it looked too nice to be something you'd wear to school. She had some sort of scarf tied tightly around her throat, and there was something drawn on the back of one of her hands, an image or symbol of some kind.

He wondered if it was a tattoo. She looked about the same age as him. Can you get a tattoo when you are under sixteen? he wondered. Is there a legal age limit?

He had once read a story in the paper about a mother in America being arrested for giving her nine-month-old baby a tattoo on its arm and the story had really irritated him. Not because he was concerned for the baby – he was, of course, everyone would have been – no, he was irritated because they hadn't said in the paper what the tattoo was of. How could you write the story of a baby getting a tattoo, he'd thought, and not tell your readers what the tattoo was?

He knew it wasn't really relevant. If you tattoo something on a baby's arm then it's terrible whatever the tattoo is. But there is also a difference between tattooing something like a flower or "I love my mum" on the kid's arm and tattooing, say, a picture of Satan or Ed Sheeran's face or a list of all the winners of the FA Cup since 1981.

He looked up and realized Cally was staring at him, waiting. He was doing it again, daydreaming. Jack regularly got into trouble for this habit.

It drove his dad crazy.

"Stop daydreaming, Jack!"

"Come back to us, Jack!"

"Earth calling Planet Duvet!"

Jack wasn't trying to annoy anyone; it was just the way he was built. It annoyed his teachers too. And so Jack had learned to be annoyed by it and when he caught himself daydreaming, he felt like he'd let himself down.

The thing was, he would pay attention if he was interested in what someone was saying. And so it followed that his teacher wasn't being interesting enough. His dad wasn't being interesting enough. In which case, it wasn't his fault at all.

"Why are you staring at my hand?" Cally asked him.

"Oh. I don't… Is that a tattoo?"

"Don't be silly," she retorted. "I was just doodling."

Cally lifted her hand and showed him.

She'd drawn an outline of a heart in red and filled it in with black ink.

"Did you *really* like her song?" snapped Cally. "Wanda's song. It was not that good. Were you pretending when you said you liked it?"

"Maybe. Yes," mumbled Jack.

From some way off there was a sound. Like water hitting a wall, like waves smacking against something solid. Two wet, slappy thunks, and then it was quiet again.

Cally looked hard at him and then closed her eyes. Jack wondered whether he should apologize. But he stayed quiet, and waited.

"I wanted her to like me," said Jack at last. "She took a risk singing it. Put herself out there. I wanted to show her that I'd ... noticed her. It feels good to be noticed."

He waited for Cally to say something.

"Sorry," said Jack.

"How can I trust you now?" Cally said, just before the room exploded.

At least, that was what it felt like. There was a loud bang, and they were knocked to the ground by what felt like a huge wave. A circular white wave that they didn't see coming, converging on them, a searingly bright light, and then sudden darkness. A strange sensation of warm water flowing over them and through them, even though they remained completely dry. The ground shuddered violently and smoke filled the space.

Jack staggered to his feet.

When the smoke cleared, he saw that

they were surrounded by four walls, a closed door in the middle of each. There was a ceiling overhead and in one corner a large desk with a man sat behind it.

The desk had a plaque on it that read **"Gary"**. The man was hunched over, his head in his hands.

He lifted his head, eyed Jack and Cally warily and, as though seeing them was the last straw, said, "Oh God."

Jack glanced at Cally. She looked even angrier than she had done moments before.

He hoped she wasn't going to make things even worse.

Jack looked around the room again. It was about as plain as a room could get. The four dark brown doors were made of varnished wood and were covered in scratches and dents, like they had been around for a long time. The walls were painted a dirty yellowy-white. There were no paintings or posters or notices. No windows. The ceiling had spotlights in it, not all of which were working. It looked like what Jack imagined an ordinary office would look like. A boring office.

"Let me guess," said Cally. There was a definite edge to her voice. **"You're Gary?"**

The man groaned and let his head fall on to the desk.

Cally shook her head in exasperation.

"Say something," she mouthed at Jack.

Jack shook his head vigorously. His gut told him to wait and see what happened. His gut *always* told him to wait and see what happened. He didn't want to be like that. He'd love to take charge and lead them through this situation they found themselves in. He'd love to be the one with the insight and the bravery and the cleverness to know exactly what to do. But the thought of making a bad move, the thought of possibly making things worse, made him freeze. He felt overwhelmed by what was happening and couldn't think clearly. He couldn't work out what

Gary wanted to hear. So best to wait and see, he thought. How could he act if he didn't know what to do? He shook his head again.

Cally rolled her eyes and turned back to the man behind the desk.

"Gary, my name's Cally. I suspect you already know that, but I'm telling you anyway out of politeness. Now, Wanda said we should meet you and find out what to do next. Are you going to tell us why we've been kidnapped and put in this room? Because that's what's happened here, isn't it? I don't know about laughing boy here" – she nodded towards Jack, who certainly was not laughing – "but I don't want to be here. I want to be *not* here. I want to be at home eating Marmite toast and watching telly. Not here looking at the top of your balding head. The hair that is left on your bonce could do with a wash, may I say. Now, answer me, Gary. Why are we here?"

Gary moved not one hair.

"Gary?" Cally asked flatly. "Gary?"

Nothing.

"Garygarygarygaryarygarygary?" she said.
"GARRRRRRRRRRYYYYYY!"

Jack was in awe of Cally's fearlessness. She was so confident.

"OK, I'm out of here," Cally declared. "This is a waste of time. I'm going home."

And she turned on her heel and walked to the nearest door.

"Where are you going?" Jack asked, trying not to sound as desperate as he felt. "You can't just leave!"

"Watch me," she said, putting her hand on the door handle.

"We're supposed to stick together."

"Let's stick together, then. Coming?"

Jack looked to Gary. Cally surely had no idea where she was going. Who knew what dangers lurked out there beyond the door?

But on the other hand, they'd been told to open doors. And Cally was right; Gary didn't seem to be much use at all.

At least Cally was doing *something*, Jack thought.

"All right," Jack said. "I'm coming."

Cally nodded and pushed down on the door handle.

The door was locked.

Cally gave it a couple of shoves but it didn't budge.

"Of course!" realized Jack. *"To get through each door, you'll need a key.* That was what

Wanda said." He turned back to the slumped figure. **"Gary, have you got a key?"**

No reply from Gary.

Cally tried the other doors. All locked.

Jack was definitely hungry now, and he wasn't good when he was hungry. He'd get grumpy and useless. He had another look around the room. There was nothing else there. Nothing but Cally and Gary and him. And the desk.

Jack wondered whether if there wasn't any food, then would there be any water?

Jack knew that lack of water was more dangerous than lack of food. You could survive quite a while without food, but not without water.

He looked again at Gary. Surely, if there were supplies of food and water, they would be in that desk.

But how could he get it? What if he couldn't? What if he got weaker and weaker? What if he got weak and Cally and Gary ganged up on him? What if they asked him which animal he was most scared of and he told them it was flamingoes because one had tried to bite him in London Zoo when he was three and they made him wear a flamingo costume in exchange for bread and they took photos of him in the flamingo costume looking really stupid and texted the pics to all his mates?

"Jack?" snapped Cally.

"I'M NOT A FLAMINGO!" yelled Jack.

Gary and Cally stared at him. There was a pause.

"Pardon?" said Cally, smiling slightly. "*What*

aren't you?"

"Um. A flamingo," said Jack sheepishly.

"OK," said Cally slowly. "Good to know. Do you want one?"

"One what?" asked Jack.

"A biscuit," said Cally, as if talking to a very young child. "Gary offered you a biscuit."

Jack looked at Gary, who was indeed holding out a packet of biscuits.

"Oh," said Jack, "yes, I would. Thank you. What sort of biscuit?"

"Does it matter?" said Cally.

"Not really," said Jack, taking one.

The three of them munched on their biscuits, which turned out to be chocolate chip cookies, without speaking.

This was mainly because Jack and Cally were looking at Gary in horror. Jack had never seen anyone eat biscuits in a more disgusting manner.

Gary placed three biscuits in each hand and slammed the six of them into each other as hard as he could, rubbing his hands together so that the biscuits crumbled on to the desk, leaving melted pieces of chocolate chip smeared over his palms.

After giving his hands a good lick and then rubbing them on his trousers, he scraped all the crumbs into a pile and pressed them together. Then he lifted the big soggy ball to his wide-open mouth and shoved it inside.

Bits of biscuit fell to the desk, chocolate smudged across his cheeks and up his nose as Gary munched loudly, mouth open.

It was revolting.

Once Gary had finished swallowing, he sighed heavily, rubbed a finger along the inside of his top teeth, inspected the wet clot of half-eaten mush that he pulled out, put the finger back into his mouth to suck off the slushy paste, picked up the biscuit packet and flicked out six more cookies.

Jack felt he should take his chance now before the process began all over again.

"Excuse me, Gary," he ventured. "Thanks for the biscuit. Can you help us?"

Gary looked irritated to be interrupted during his cookie ceremony.

"What do you want?" he said moodily.

"Well, what do we do?"

"Go through the Rooms," he said. "Didn't Wanda tell you?"

"Sort of. Where do we start?"

Gary pointed to the door to his right. "Try that door."

"Oh," said Jack, slightly surprised that it had been that easy. "Thanks."

Jack went over and tried the handle. The door was still locked.

"The door's locked," said Jack.

"Yes," said Gary.

"Do you have a key, please, Gary?" asked Cally.

"You're supposed to work out where it is. There's a riddle," said Gary. "I wrote it."

"Oh, right," said Jack.

Gary cleared his throat noisily. "I will say

this only once. Listen carefully."

"Will do," said Jack.

"My first," began Gary, "is in **DESK** but not in **CHURCH**."

"Oh no! I hate these kind of puzzles," moaned Cally. "They're so confusing."

"Shh," hissed Jack.

"My first," repeated a peeved Gary, "is in **DESK** but not in **CHURCH**. My second is in **DESK** but not in **BURP**."

Jack frowned.

"My third is in **DESK** but not in **TARPAULIN**."

Gary leaned back in his chair.

"My fourth is in **DESK** but not in **COLLYWOBBLES**."

There was a pause.

"Is the answer . . . 'desk'?" asked Jack.

"Yes," said Gary, reaching into the desk and

pulling out a key. "Here you go." He belched. "Now I think about it," he continued, "that was probably a bit too easy."

"We don't mind easy," said Cally quickly. "Very happy with easy."

"It won't always be that easy," said Gary. Or at least they thought that was what he had said, but they couldn't be sure because he was cramming a handful of custard creams into his mouth.

He put the key on the desk. It was sticky with wet biscuit pap and saliva.

Jack and Cally looked at each other.

"OK, fine," said Jack after a moment, and he grabbed it.

They went over to the door, inserted the key and the lock opened.

"Do we take the key with us?" said Jack.

"You can't," replied Gary. And he was right; the key wouldn't budge from the door.

"How many rooms will there be?" asked Cally.

"I'M EATING BISCUITS," Gary yelled, suddenly sounding very cross.

Jack and Cally took the hint, opened the door and walked through it.

The room did not feel like a room. It looked like a corridor. It was only the width of the door through which they had just come, the ceiling was low, and the passageway stretched so far away from them they couldn't see its end.

On the right, a few paces along, was a door marked **EXIT** . Jack tried the handle, but it was locked.

"Should we walk, do you think?" asked Jack.

Just then, they heard footsteps. Coming into view from a long, long way down the corridor was a small man in a long, white, flowing robe. He was walking as quickly as he could towards them, but he had a lot of distance to cover and his legs were small. He was muttering to himself. His long hair was also white and flapped behind him as he walked.

"Whoever this is better not try anything funny," murmured Cally to Jack.

The white-robed man walked towards them with his head bowed. He carried a big book, also white. Once he got to within a few paces of Jack and Cally, he stopped abruptly, placed the book on the ground, knelt, put his forehead on the book and slowly lifted his legs into the air.

"He's doing a headstand," whispered Jack.

"I can see that, you berk," muttered Cally. **"This is already annoying me."**

They waited.

The little man let out a deep sigh and lowered himself down from his headstand. His long hair had fallen forward over his eyes and he had to sweep it back over his head. Jack realized with a start that it wasn't hair from his head, but very long eyebrow hair that he swept back over his bald pate.

The man strode towards them. He was tiny; he only came up to their waists at most. He looked very cross.

He opened his book and flicked through its pages.

Cally opened her mouth to say something, but the little man looked up sharply as if to say, *No you don't, madam.*

She bit her lip.

While he riffled through page after page of the book, getting increasingly agitated as he did so, it gave Jack a moment to examine the curious eyebrow-hair arrangement that the small man had going on. The hair was incredible.

Long enough to sweep up from his eyebrows, over his head and down the back of his skull to the collar of his gown. Jack reckoned it was almost as long as an arm. And it was growing out of his eyebrows!

Having a hairline that started right above his eyes was startling. He had absolutely no visible forehead. It looked as if he was wearing a cheap wig that had slipped forward and was about to slither right down and cover his eyes.

Jack noticed that, as the man was becoming more frantic looking for whatever he was trying to find in his book, his hair was separating in the middle and beginning to slide off the two sides of his shiny bald head towards his ears.

The man must have felt this happening because he abruptly stopped scanning the book, lifted a hand to his head and felt the exposed piece of scalp. He turned away, flicked all the hair forward off his head and over his face, brought both his hands up to his mouth under this hair-curtain and, with a remarkable amount of noise, hacking, hocking and snorting, dragged up every ounce of phlegm from every corner of his body, spat vigorously into each hand, smeared it across his shiny head, waited for a moment, then flicked the hair back up over his head and patted it down with his hands. Once he was satisfied he'd managed to stick the hair down successfully, he turned back to Jack and Cally, picked up the book and, without looking at them, continued to scan through it.

All Jack could think was, *Please don't touch me, just please don't touch me.*

The man slammed the book shut, closed his eyes and tilted his head back. Then he said:

"Ubarube yuboubu cruboss?"

Cally frowned.

"Sorry?"

The little man looked irritated. **"Ubit's uba subimplube qubuestubion!"** he said, **"Ubarube yuboubu cruboss?"**

"Nope, sorry, what?" said Cally.

This sent the man into a total meltdown. **"Whuby ubarube subo ubannuboyubing!!!!"** he shouted.

The little man threw the book to the floor and gave it a kick. It skidded across the hard, white floor and stopped at Jack's feet. This made him even angrier.

"MUBY BUBOOK!!!" he yelled at Cally. **"DUBON'T DUBAMUBAGUBE UBIT!!!"**

"WHY ARE YOU SHOUTING AT ME!!! I HAVEN'T DONE ANYTHING!!"

"UBOH RUBEUBALLY!?" he shouted in her face.

He ran over, picked up the book and marched off the way he'd come.

"Come on," said Jack, setting off after the man. "We need the key."

"He's talking gibberish."

"I know," said Jack. "But we don't have any choice."

Jack caught up with the man. "Er, excuse me. I think we got off on the wrong foot..."

"GUBET LUBOST!!" shouted the man back.

"Can we have a key, please?" asked Jack.

"UBASK MUBE PRUBOPUBERLUBY!"

"Why is your eyebrow hair so disgusting?" asked Cally.

This sent the man into his biggest meltdown yet. He threw his book down and stomped towards Cally. Jack thought the man might pop, he was so red and angry.

"It's revolting," said Cally. "All that spit smeared over his head. Yuk!"

"YUBOU UBARUBE RUBUDE!" he snarled at Cally.

"Wait! Are you calling me rude?" she asked.

"YUBES!!" shouted the little man, looking suddenly delighted. **"RUBUDE!"**

"Rude is rubude," said Cally. "It's a code!" She pointed at herself. "Rubude?"

"YUBES!" said the man delightedly, doing a little jig that involved hitching up his robe and prancing around. His hairy little feet were stuffed into sandals way too small for him.

"And yubes is . . . 'yes'," said Cally.

"Look at his hairy ankles," said Jack quietly to Cally. "He looks like a goat down there. That's making me anxious."

"Help me work this out! If rubude is rude and yubes is yes. . ."

"He smells a bit like a goat now we're near him. I don't like goats."

"Got it!" shouted Cally, "Cuban. . .?"

"Although he can't be a goat because he's

69

wearing sandals."

Cally was frowning with concentration.

"Wube. . ." she continued.

"You never see goats in sandals."

"Hubave..."

"At least *I've* never seen a goat in sandals."

"Thube . . . kubey?" Cally finished.

The effect of these words on the little man was startling.

"YUBES!" said the little man, clapping delightedly. **"YUBES!"**

Cally looked thrilled.

"What did you say?" asked Jack.

The man threw himself forward into a handstand, causing his gown to fall down and reveal more of his hairy legs, his underwear (pants with **BUBIG BUBOY** written on them) and his back, which was so hairy no skin was visible.

He worked off one of the sandals with his other foot and it dropped to the floor. There, on the sole of his bare foot, was a key. With a flick of his foot, the key fell to the floor in front of Jack and Cally.

They looked at each other. Neither wanted to pick up a key which had been stored under this man's hairy foot.

"I worked it out, you pick up the key," said Cally.

Jack sighed and did so.

"You put 'ub' before each vowel sound," she grinned, "So you are 'Juback', I'm 'Cuballuby'. Quite pleased with myself for getting that."

Jack opened the door marked EXIT .

"You're pretty smart when you're not angry," he said to her.

"I can be smart *and* angry," said Cally, then calling back to the little man, still in a handstand, "Bubye bubye, hubairuby muban!"

They walked through the door, hearing **"HUBELP MUBE! UBI'M STUBUCK!"** just before it clicked shut.

They found themselves back in the room with Gary.

"Ugh," said Cally. "You again. I thought we were going on a journey."

"Rude," said Gary, reaching for a packet of chocolate bourbons. "So you and Gub didn't kill each other then?" he continued, sounding surprised.

"He's *very* angry, isn't he?" said Cally, blithely. "Imagine getting that angry! What's the point? Where next?"

Jack decided it best not to challenge Cally on her apparent lack of self-awareness. As usual, he decided saying nothing was the easiest option. He was actually a little envious that Cally was able to express her feelings so freely, even if those emotions nearly always seemed to be anger.

"Shall we get on? May we have the next key please, Gary?" asked Jack.

"Sure. You just have to answer this question," said Gary. "What do you call a French man wearing sandals?"

"Phillipe Phillop," said Jack. "That's such a dad joke."

"I thought it was funny," said Gary, handing them a key.

"I don't get it," said Cally, as she and Jack pushed open the door to which Gary had pointed.

They stepped into a large, high-ceilinged, dark room. In the centre were about twenty people arranged in a line in height order, shortest on the left, tallest on the right. The youngest, a boy wearing a Led Zeppelin T-shirt, was probably about twelve; the oldest looked *very* old. They were all smiling manically.

"Give me an H!" shouted the smallest in the line, a man with pink hair and glasses, wearing a nightshirt that reached the floor.

"H!" shouted back the group.

"Give me an E!" the pink-haired man yelled.

"E!" yelled back the group.

"Give me an L!"

"L!"

"Give me another L!"

"L!"

"Give me another L!"

76

"That's too many L's, Bernard," whispered the girl standing next to him.

"Sorry, yes – **give me an O!**"

"O!"

"What have you got?"

"HELLO!" they shouted merrily.

"Hi," said Jack quickly. Cally said nothing.

"You are Jack and Cally, yes?" asked Bernard.

"That's right," said Jack.

"Great!" said Bernard. **"Give me a J!"**

"J!" the group yelled.

"Give me an A!"

"A!"

"Give me a C!"

"Wait!" shouted Cally. "Are you going to spell out *Jack* and *Cally*?"

"Yes!" grinned Bernard.

"You don't need to do that," said Cally curtly.

"Oh, all right," said Bernard. Jack thought he looked quite deflated.

"We have a new carpet," said a pale, toothy woman. **"Would you like to smell it?"**

"Er, you're OK," said Cally, "but thanks anyway."

"Are you sure?" asked Bernard. "It smells great, doesn't it, everyone?"

The people murmured their agreement enthusiastically.

"Would you mind if *we* smelled it?" asked the man.

"Um . . . go ahead," said Jack.

At that the whole row of people fell to the ground and pressed their noses to the carpet.

"My new favourite smell!" one piped up enthusiastically from the floor.

"Mine too!" said another.

"Are you sure you don't want to have a sniff?" the man persisted. "You won't regret it."

"I really don't want to smell it," said Cally.

"But thanks for the offer," said Jack as pleasantly as he could.

"I see," said the man, grinning extravagantly. "I see. Everyone up."

It took a few of the older ones some time to stand upright, and there was a lot of wincing and face-pulling as they did so.

"Gary sent us," said Cally. "Do you have a key?"

That question had quite an effect on the line of people. It seemed to make them nervous. The pale toothy woman started to blink rapidly and Bernard went pale.

"Give me a Y!" shouted Bernard.

"Y!" yelled the group.

"Give me an E!"

"E!"

"Give me an S!"

"S!"

"What have you got?"

"*Yes*," interrupted Cally. "You've got *yes*. Bernard, you don't have to do the spelling-out thing every time."

"Sorry," said Bernard, "I'm a bit anxious. So, we do have the key. But first we have to ask you a teeny-weeny riddle and if you ..." Bernard mumbled something they couldn't quite hear.

"... then you get the key."

"Sorry, Bernard," said Jack politely. "Didn't

quite catch the middle bit. If we *what* then we get the key?"

"If you manage not to be ..." Bernard mumbled something incomprehensible again. "**... then you get the key!**"

"**Louder, Bernie!**" shouted Cally. "I'm getting annoyed!"

"What Bernard is too nice to say," explained the pale, toothy woman, "is that if you can answer the riddle correctly, then you can have the key. If not, you will be mauled to death by the small lions or poisoned to death by the Brazilian wandering spiders."

"**What?!?**" shouted Cally. "Can't we just have the key?"

"**I am so, so, so, so, so, so, so, so, so, so sorry, but no. You have to pass the test,**" said Bernard, apologetically.

"Fair enough," said Jack.

"*Fair enough?*" yelled Cally. **"I don't want to be eaten by small lions or poisoned by spiders!"**

"Press the button, Tony," said Bernard, and the second tallest boy with the big, curly hair bent down and pushed a small red button on the floor.

Four thick glass panels dropped from above, narrowly missing Cally and Jack and boxing them in.

Before they could so much as cry out, the section of floor they were standing on shot up into the air about five metres, taking them and the glass walls with it.

Two sections of floor on either side of them dropped a similar distance creating two pits,

each about the size of a boxing ring, one below
them on their left, one on their right.

The pit on the left began to fill with spiders.
Large, brown, hairy spiders. Jack figured each

one was about as big as his face. And there were thousands of them, crawling over, under and around each other.

"Not spiders," Jack heard Cally say under her breath. "Please not spiders."

Jack looked over to the other pit. It was filling with small lions. They looked as though big lions had been shrunk to the size of a regular pet cat. They were actually pretty cute, thought Jack. They roared at a very high pitch, like they'd inhaled some helium. They were almost funny.

Almost.

"What's happening?" Jack shouted to Bernard, trying to keep calm.

84

"Right, well, firstly we are *terribly* sorry about all this. Truly. And, secondly, I should say that in one pit you have a large number of Brazilian wandering spiders. Incredibly venomous, possibly the most dangerous spiders on the planet – a bite from just one could kill you, so we've really overdone it here with so many!"

He chuckled nervously and the rest of the group laughed along too.

"The *lions*, on the other hand," Bernard went on. "They look cute, don't they! **So cute!** Those little squeaky roars! Adorable. But no. They are starving, absolutely famished, haven't been fed for ages those fellas and they will, well, eat you. It'll be messy."

"Didn't you say something about a riddle?"

asked Jack. Cally was still staring at the spiders.

"Yes!" said Bernard. **"Ready? Here it is. You need to tell us something. If it's false, then you'll be dropped into the pit of spiders. If it's true—"**

"We get the key!" exclaimed Jack.

"Afraid not," said Bernard. **"If the statement is true, you get dropped into the lion pit."**

"Wait," said Jack, "if the statement is *false* we get the spiders, and if the statement is *true* we get the lions? **How can we win?!"**

Bernard beamed. "I was coming to that. If you can tell us something that is *neither* true nor false, then you get the key. **Got it?"**

"Not really," moaned Cally.

"How will you know if a statement is true or false?" asked Jack. "I mean if my statement is 'I have a pet rabbit called Bunny Delight' – how do you know if it's true or not?"

"Is it true?"

"Yes."

"Then into the lions you go."

"What if I was lying?"

"Then you'd go into the spiders. You die in the spiders or you die in the lions."

"Or we get the key?"

"Oh, yes, or you get the key. Hahaha!"

"Right," said Jack, adding a little sarcastically, "thanks."

"You're welcome!" said Bernard brightly. "Take your time! Think about it. Relax. You've got at least two minutes before we need your statement."

He gave them a big thumbs up.

Jack turned to Cally.

"What we going to do?" asked Jack quietly.

"We've only got two minutes."

Cally was silent. Jack saw that she was shaking. All her bravado was gone.

"Cally?"

"This is my nightmare," she whispered. **"My absolute worst nightmare. I'm going to be dropped into a pit of deadly spiders."**

"You're not," said Jack as calmly as he could.

"I knew it," she said. "I've been scared of spiders my whole life and now they've got me."

Jack grabbed her by the arms.

"Snap out of it! You don't have to end up in there," he said. "We only go in the pit of spiders if we tell a lie."

"Oh great!" said Cally. "Let's tell the truth and then we can get thrown to the hungry lions. Result!"

Jack looked over to the group of people.

They weren't watching. They were too busy smelling their carpet.

"How can a statement be neither true nor false?" he asked Cally.

Bernard lifted his head from the carpet and looked up at Jack and Cally.

"You have about thirty seconds left! Thanks ever so much!"

"Jack!" cried Cally. **"Do something! Do something, please!"**

Jack took some deep breaths and tried to focus.

"Wait. . ." he said. "We will be dropped into the spiders if we tell a *lie*. So, if we say 'We will be dropped into the spiders' that will be true. In which case we should be dropped to the lions." He clutched his head. This was painfully confusing.

"That's it!" exclaimed Jack. "Our statement should be: 'We will be dropped into the spiders'. Then they can't drop us into the spiders because then the statement would be *true*. But they can't drop us into the lions either because that makes the statement 'We will be dropped into the spiders' *false*. Which means we should be dropped into the spiders for telling a lie. The statement is neither true or false."

Cally nodded slowly. **"I think that's right,"** she whispered. "But if you're wrong then we get dropped into the spider pit."

They stared at each other. "Do we have a choice?" said Jack. "Got a better idea?"

"No."

"So, we have to do it."

Cally jumped up.

"Hey! Carpet people!" she yelled.

"Aloha!" waved the pale, toothy woman. "Honestly you want to get a nose-full of this carpet. Sensational."

The group stopped smelling the carpet and formed their line again.

Cally took one last look at the heaving mass of spiders below her. Thousands of them, writhing over each other, scuttling around the pit, their long, hairy legs propelling them swiftly this way and that. A living, moving, pulsating furry mass. A squirming carpet of death.

Cally took a deep breath.

"We will be dropped into the spiders," she said.

The group stopped smiling. The pale, toothy woman gasped.

"Say that again," said Bernard, after a

moment.

"We ..." repeated Cally, sounding more nervous, "... will be dropped into the spiders."

The group stood motionless.

"Well?" asked Jack.

"Well what?" said Bernard.

"What happens now? Did we manage it?"

"You did it," said Bernard. **"That's the right answer."**

Jack punched the air. Cally punched the glass wall.

"Can we have the key then?" she asked.

"I guess," said Bernard. "Can I just say that obviously we're glad you escaped, but we really wanted you to smell our carpet. Tony, press the button."

Tony bent down and pressed the button. Once he did so, the pit containing the spiders dropped down rapidly like a lift descending and the floor closed over the top. The same with the pit of small lions, their high-pitched roars fading into the distance.

The platform on which Jack and Cally were standing lowered, the glass walls flew up and away.

"Shall we smell the carpet now?" Jack asked.

"Too late," Bernard said huffily.

Bernard pulled the key from his pocket. He looked at it, shrugged and placed it on the ground. Then he and the group turned away.

Jack darted forward and picked up the key, feeling pleased with himself. That was some impressively clear thinking given the circumstances. Cally hadn't been much help, but he couldn't really blame her as she'd been so terrified.

They went back through the door they'd entered through. It said EXIT above it.

There, again, was Gary. He'd built a model of the Eiffel Tower out of bourbon biscuits.

"Hello, Gary. Again," said Cally.

"I feel bad we didn't smell their carpet," Jack said. "They really wanted us to."

"Why should we?" Cally retorted.

"I don't know. If it would have made them happy, why not?"

"Those spiders. Weren't you frightened?"

"Of course," Jack said.

"You didn't seem to be. You were totally calm."

"Well," Jack half-laughed. "I suppose I was."

"We were on the verge of death; you were totally calm."

"What are you trying to say?"

"I'm saying it's really suspicious!" Cally was getting worked up. "**It's really weird!** Those spiders, we were moments from death."

"I'm not as frightened of spiders as you are."

"You're not frightened of dying?!"

"I *was* frightened."

"Then why not show it? Only two reasons I can think of." She put her hands on her hips. **"You're in on this, or you're a robot."**

"A robot?! What?!"

"You have no feelings!"

"I have feelings," retorted Jack. "What do you mean? That's ... I just worked out that problem. You know nothing about me. How can you call me a robot? You have no idea who I am."

"You feel nothing," insisted Cally. "You're a robot."

"I am not! Why are you doing this?"

"Well go on, what have you had to deal with?"

"You, right now."

"I knew it! Nothing, you've had nothing!"

"Stop saying that."

"Name one bad thing that's ever happened to you. . ."

"Why should I? We just escaped..."

"I don't trust you! You're weird! Who are you? Why are you all messing with my head?

You're probably a pampered little mummy's boy who's been wrapped in cotton wool your whole life!"

"My mum died."

There was a silence.

Cally stared at him.

"My mum died," Jack continued. "Exactly a year ago. So that's something bad that happened to me. **Happy now?**"

He looked at the ground and clenched his fists.

Cally was looking at the ground too.

"I haven't spoken to anyone about it before and I don't want to speak to you about it. I don't know why I mentioned it, so forget I said it."

He shifted his weight.

"I don't want to talk about it. Don't tell me I've had it easy. Don't tell me I can't feel anything. You don't know me."

Cally was taken aback.

Jack could feel tears starting to come. He swallowed and tried to hold them back. He didn't want to cry in front of Gary and Cally.

The silence was broken by Gary popping the top of the Eiffel Tower into his mouth and chomping loudly.

Jack and Cally turned to him.

"I'm eating biscuits," said Gary, cramming in more biscuits.

"We can see that," said Cally. "Can we have another key, please?"

"OK, you have to solve a riddle to get the key. I've made this one harder. What tastes better than it smells?"

"What tastes better than it smells?" said Cally. "Cheese? Cheese can smell disgusting but it can still taste all right."

"Nope," said Gary.

Cally glanced at Jack, who was still staring at the floor.

"What smells bad?" she said. "Feet? Smelly feet?"

"Why would you taste smelly feet?" said Gary.

"OH, I DON'T KNOW," Cally shouted, losing patience. "This is stupid."

"What tastes better than it smells?" said Jack quietly. "A tongue."

Cally stared at him. "Oh yeah," she said.

"Nice!" said Gary. "You're good at this."

He reached into his desk and tossed them a key, pointing to a door. Cally unlocked the door and, without hesitation, she and Jack stepped through it together.

They found themselves in a low-ceilinged living room. Beams on the roof, a sofa and two comfortable armchairs, a log fire burning in the fireplace. The room had two windows which, beyond a small neat garden, looked out on to pretty countryside with fields and trees. In front of the fire lay a black dog, asleep on a rug, and above the fire a mantelpiece with framed photos of smiling adults and children.

The room was cosy. *Someone old lives here*, thought Jack. It smelled of old.

"Sorry about your mum," said Cally.

"It's fine," said Jack. "You weren't to know."

"I didn't mean to shout. Sorry. I'm glad you're here." She hesitated. "I get angry easily. Lately."

"I understand," said Jack. "I get angry too. I got angry at my dad just before I came here."

"Why?"

"He was … taking pictures of me," Jack said. "At the funfair. Now that I say it out loud, it doesn't sound that bad."

Jack tried to think why having his photo taken annoyed him so much. It wasn't just that it took ages. Or that he had to smile when he didn't feel like smiling. He was used to pretending he felt one thing when he really felt something completely different.

It was something to do with being pinned down. A photo is a permanent record: a permanent record of Jack at that moment. A photo of Jack now captured him as he didn't want to be captured. It fixed a record of *this* Jack, and Jack hoped that *this* Jack was only temporary. This Jack was sad and quiet and afraid of everything. He wanted to get back to the happier Jack, the more confident Jack, the Jack he liked. He didn't want a photographic reminder of his sadness and his fake smile standing beside his dad with *his* sadness and *his* fake smile.

"It just annoyed me," Jack shrugged.

"Everything annoys me," said Cally. **"Including you, sometimes."**

They stood quietly for a moment.

"Shall we look for the key?"

Jack sighed. "Every time we get the key, we just end up back with Gary. We need to find another way out."

He walked over to the window and tried to open it. Locked.

"Do you think the dog has the key?" he said.

"Ask it," said Cally with half a smile.

Jack walked up to the dog. "It's asleep."

"So?"

"So, I don't want to wake it. I don't like people waking *me* up when I'm asleep."

"Then I'll do it." Cally strolled over to the dog and was just about to yell in its ear when the dog looked up at her and said, **"Don't do it."**

It then laid its head down again and went back to sleep.

Cally stood open-mouthed. She turned to Jack.

"Did you...?"

But before she could finish her question, the door opened and in walked two old men. The first was tall with long grey hair that hung smartly down over his shoulders. He wore a sleeveless zip-up fleece over a checked shirt. The second, shorter with a full moustache and dressed in a navy blue V-neck sweater straining around his belly, was carrying an empty tray.

"Sit," said the first.

Cally and Jack sat on the sofa.

"Stand," said the second.

They stood up again.

"I'm Deuce," said the long-haired, tall one, "and he's a liar," he said, motioning to the other old man.

"I'm Bruce," said the short, moustachioed one. "He's the liar, not me."

"Am not," said Deuce.

"Am too," said Bruce.

"Sit," said Deuce.

They all sat.

"Stand," said Bruce.

They all stood.

There was a pause and the four of them stood there looking at each other. The dog started twitching and whimpering in its sleep. Cally eyed it warily.

"You win, Deuce," said Bruce. **"Let's sit."**

They all sat down. Bruce put the empty tray on his lap and drummed his fingers on it.

"I'm Cally and that's Jack," said Cally.

"So?" said Deuce.

"Be nice, Deuce," Bruce snapped at Deuce, drumming his fingers even harder on the tray. **"Be nice."**

"Sorry," said Deuce, "I apologize. So, what can we do you for?"

"We need you to give us a key," said Jack. "There's usually some sort of test."

Bruce and Deuce were silent. "Um … I noticed something," said Jack after a bit. "I noticed you both said the other was a liar. Is this one of those riddles, where we have to work out which one of you is lying and which one is telling the truth by asking you a question?"

Deuce and Bruce continued to say nothing. The dog shuddered and whimpered but didn't wake up. "Well, OK . . . let me think, this could be interesting," continued Jack. "One always lies, one tells the truth."

"Are you a liar, Deuce?" said Cally bluntly.

"Nope," said Deuce.

"There you go, he's not the liar, Bruce is the liar. Easy. Key please."

"He could be lying about being the liar," said Jack. "They'll both say no to that question. The truth-teller will say, honestly, he's not the liar and the liar will lie and say he's not the liar either. Bruce, are you the liar?"

"Nope," said Bruce.

"There you go, that doesn't help."

"Oh. That's annoying," moaned Cally. "That's really annoying!"

"We need the key and . . . there *is* a key?" Jack asked.

"Yes," said Bruce and Deuce at the same time.

"Great, so there must be a logical way of working it out. I'm sure I remember this problem from school," mused Jack. "It's something to do with asking one of them what the other would say. . ."

"Wait!" jumped in Cally. "You asked them if there was a key and they both said 'yes'!"

"Exactly, we need to work out which is the liar so we can get it."

"No, don't you see? If they both said there's a key then they are either both lying or both telling the truth!"

"Oh," said Jack, the wind taken out of his

sails. "Oh yeah."

"We're not the riddle," said Bruce.

"We're not," said Deuce.

"Oh. That's a shame," said Jack.

Cally grinned. "Remember what Gary said? It's not as easy as it looks."

"Yeah, we're not the riddle," repeated Bruce. "I just think he's a liar."

"We still need the key," said Jack.

"You need to help us out first," said Bruce, the light from the fire flickering off his shiny forehead. "We have a little problem we need your help with."

He pulled what looked like a small brown nut from his pocket.

"This," he said, "is a small brown nut called the kiken nut. Do you know why it's called the kiken nut?"

"Is this the riddle?" asked Cally.

"No, we'll tell you when we get to the riddle part," said Deuce huffily.

"Is it because it's 'kicking' – really tasty?" suggested Jack.

"No. Kiken is Japanese for danger. This is a very dangerous nut. If you popped this little beauty in your mouth, you'd be dead in seconds."

"Luckily we just had some biscuits," said Cally drily. "So we're not hungry, thank you very much."

"On the other hand," Bruce continued, "cooked correctly, this is said to be the most exquisite food on Earth. It is highly revered in Japan; people pay hundreds and thousands of dollars for just one nut. Partly because of the taste, partly because they are so incredibly rare. A kiken tree produces only one nut every hundred years."

"And we have one," Deuce said, his eyes shining.

"Well that's terrific," said Cally, "but how can we help?"

"You are going to cook it for us," said Bruce. "You are going to cook it in that fire."

The logs in the fire crackled and spat.

"Sure, we can do that," said Jack cautiously. "What do we do?"

"You have to cook the nut for exactly forty-five

minutes and at a very high temperature. Cook it any less, it will be underdone, and an underdone kiken nut is highly poisonous. It will kill anyone who eats even a tiny portion of it. Cook it too long and it will be just as lethal. There will be an adverse chemical reaction between the amino acids, the enzymes and the natural sugar in the nut, which will create a highly toxic substance."

"But get it just right," chipped in Deuce, **"and it'll change your life. Your taste buds won't know what's hit them. You will love it."**

"All the same, I think I'll give it a miss," said Jack. "I don't care if it tastes amazing if it might kill me."

"Well, here's the thing," said Deuce in a voice so low and deep that Jack could feel his whole body vibrate. "We do. And we have the key that'll get you out of here. So you have no real choice, my friends. You need to cook the nut."

Jack and Cally looked at each other.

"I'll cook a nut, why not?" said Cally. "What have we got to lose?"

"Terrific!" exclaimed Bruce, clapping his hands together in delight. "Oh, and one other thing. You'll get to try it too!"

"Oh right," gulped Jack, the blood draining from his face. **"We have to eat it too?"**

"Of course! You are our guests; we'd never be so rude as to sit down in front of guests and eat without offering them food! That would be most uncivilized!"

Cally narrowed her eyes. "So we are the guinea pigs, to see if the nut is cooked? We die first if it isn't."

"One other thing we should mention," said Deuce. "We don't have a clock or watch or indeed anything that tells the time."

"Then how are we supposed to know when forty-five minutes have passed?" said Cally.

Bruce pulled two ropes of roughly the same length from underneath the armchair in which he was sitting and held them aloft.

"Ropes?" said Cally. "How can we tell the time with ropes?"

"You can't tell the time with them but you can *measure* time with them," said Bruce. "If you light one end of the rope, it will burn from one end to the other, and each rope will take exactly one hour to do so."

"I've got it!" said Cally. "You cut a rope exactly in half and burn one bit – that's half an hour, thirty minutes. And you cut the other half in half again. Half of thirty is fifteen. So when the first bit finishes burning after thirty minutes, you light one of the short bits, that burns for fifteen minutes. That's thirty plus fifteen – forty-five minutes. I'm a genius, let's get cooking! **It's nut time!**"

"It's not as simple as that, I'm afraid," said Bruce. "You see, these ropes do not burn at a constant rate. Sometimes they burn quickly, at other times more slowly. They definitely take an hour to burn all the way from one end to the other but that's the only thing you can rely on."

"You could risk it if you want," suggested Deuce unhelpfully. **"It's your funeral."**

He chuckled to himself at his little joke.

"Any questions?"

"When we start cooking, we just put the nut on the fire?"

"Yes, there's a special kiken nut holder we built." Bruce pointed to the fire and sure enough there was a metal device for holding something small over the flames. "Make sure the fire's going at a good lick and place the nut in the holder and you're good. We're going for a nap. See you in forty-five minutes. Or thereabouts."

"Hope you don't kiken the bucket!" said Deuce. "Catch you later."

And the two men got up and went out.

Cally sprang up and tried the door handle as soon as the door closed. Locked.

She spun around.

"OK, genius, what do we do?"

"I don't know," Jack said anxiously. He

picked up one of the ropes. "If the ropes don't burn evenly then we have no way of knowing when half an hour or quarter of an hour has passed. Maybe they just want us dead. But that doesn't make any sense. . ."

"Oh, you're dead," said a voice from near the fire. **"You're so dead."**

Cally and Jack nearly jumped out of their skins.

"Who was that?" whispered Jack. "Was that—"

"I'd give it up if I were you," the dog said. He stretched and yawned. **"I don't think you're smart enough to work it out."**

The dog had a silky smooth, chocolatey voice, gentle and urbane. He held his nose slightly in the air, which gave him a disdainful appearance.

"Aren't you supposed to be man's best friend?" said Cally.

"I don't see any men here," sniffed the dog.

"What's your name?" asked Jack, anxious to make peace with the creature.

"Jeff Onions," replied the dog. "Pleased to meet you."

"Pleased to meet you too, Mr Onions."

"Call me Jeff."

"Jeff. I'm Jack, that's Cally. Are you able to help us?"

"No," Jeff said.

"Right."

"I can tell you one thing, though I'm not sure it'll help."

"Well, we'll take anything at this point."

"There are more chickens than people in England."

Jack and Cally looked at each other, at the rope, at the fire, at the nut, then back to Jeff Onions.

"How does that help us?" asked Jack.

"Like I said, it doesn't. It's just a fact I heard earlier that I found interesting. Take it or leave it. But that's a lot of chickens. Now you better get on with the mission because they won't give you all day. They can get quite grumpy, Bruce and Deuce. I'm going to lie down again and have another nap. **See ya, wouldn't wanna be ya.**"

Jeff Onions laid himself down, yawned ostentatiously, and closed his eyes.

Jack raised his eyebrows at Cally who just shook her head.

Jack had another look at the rope he was holding.

"Do you think we should just light it and see what happens?"

There was what sounded like a snort of derision from Jeff.

"I don't think that'll help," said Cally, ignoring the dog. "We need a plan before we light anything."

Jack sighed.

"Which end are you supposed to light?" asked Cally.

"Um. . ." Jack looked at both ends of the rope he was holding. "They look identical. I suppose you could light either end."

"What happens if you light both?" said Cally.

"The two ends would both burn towards

each other, I imagine."

"**Wait, yes!** The whole rope takes an hour to burn. If we burn it twice as fast by lighting both ends, it will take exactly half an hour to burn out."

"Right, yes, yes, that's a start," said Jack, "We light both ends and it'll burn through in thirty minutes. And that's one rope gone. How do we measure fifteen minutes with the other rope though?"

"Yes, we need a half hour rope, then we could light both ends of that and get fifteen minutes."

Cally paced up and down, palms on her forehead. Jack sat on the edge of the armchair. Jeff Onions slyly opened one eye to look at them.

"That's it!" Jack exclaimed. **"You genius! You've got it!"** He was so excited he bounced up and down.

"I am?" asked Cally. "What have I done?"

"You said 'we need a half hour rope' so we can burn both ends of it. We can make a half hour rope! At the same time as we light both ends of the first rope, we light *one* end of the other. We know the first rope will take half an hour to burn through with both ends lit, so when it does, we know our second rope has also been burning for thirty minutes and has exactly thirty minutes of rope left. It's now our thirty-minute rope! At precisely that moment, we light the other end of the second rope and we know it'll take fifteen minutes to burn. That fifteen plus the thirty will get us exactly to forty-five minutes!"

"I *am* a genius!" yelled Cally. "I just didn't know it! Now we just need something to light the ropes with."

Jeff Onions lifted his head. **"Not that much of a genius,"** he drawled and looked pointedly at the fire.

"Oh yes," realized Cally. **"Fair enough. Back to sleep, you, we've got a nut to cook!"**

Jack gathered the ropes so that three of the four ends lined up and then knelt in front of the fire. Cally picked up the nut as carefully and as delicately as she could, holding it with a tissue.

"Right, are you ready?" asked Jack. "On my count of three, I'll light both ends of one rope and one end of the other, and you put the nut in the holder."

"Here we go ... one ... two ... three!"

The ropes started to fizzle and pop the moment Jack held them to the flames and, sure enough, each end started to burn. They were definitely burning at very different speeds. One end of the first rope was disappearing fast as the flame ate it up, the other end hardly moved.

Jack laid them down on the floor tiles in front of the fire. The nut sat securely in its cradle. All seemed to be going to plan.

Cally smiled. They sat in silence for a moment.

"Are you going to tell me why you are here?" said Jack after a bit.

"I don't know why I'm here."

"No, but ... there must be a reason we've been put together. Why we keep having to go through the Rooms. Be good to find out why, wouldn't it?"

Cally shrugged, stared into the fire and said nothing.

"I'll start then," Jack began, cautiously, **"Maybe ... if what links us..."**

The words caught in his throat; tears pricked his eyes. He gave himself a second to gather his thoughts.

"Look, like I said – my mum died. I'm really confused about it. I don't know if I'm feeling the right things."

He glanced at Cally. She was still looking into the fire. He pressed on.

"Sometimes I'm heartbroken," he said. "Other times it seems fine. I don't understand that. I just want to talk to someone who can tell me it's normal to feel like that. It's been a year and I don't know if I'm supposed to be over it or if I should be more upset. I worry about both. Sometimes when it's really bad I feel like I want to run away and never come back, but then what good would that do because I'd still be with myself? I can't run away from myself, and sometimes I want to. I can't turn my mind off. I wake up in the night after a bad dream and I'd do anything to be out of my head. To step outside my head and go somewhere else. I know that probably doesn't make sense. **Is that normal?**"

Cally said nothing.

"My dad refuses to talk about it. He just says, 'Let's be brave,' and then changes the subject. So, I feel like I'm not being brave and I'm wallowing because I keep thinking about it. But why won't he talk about it? It's like he's ashamed so I feel ashamed. I keep waiting for things to get better but they don't. **Do I have to be like this for ever?** At least with this stupid nut you know how long it's supposed to take. I don't know how long it's supposed to take for me to work out how to deal with my mum dying."

The log fire hissed and crackled.

"Anyway," Jack said quietly. "Whatever."

He stood up and walked over to the window. It was a beautiful sunny day out there. The grass on the lawn looked like it had been freshly cut, there were loads of colourful flowers, and high in the sky two birds circled slowly. *Where are we?* thought Jack. No buildings in sight.

He came back to the fire.

"Does that feel like it's been thirty minutes?" Jack asked.

Cally shrugged.

"Dunno, but that second rope has hardly burned at all."

She was right. Although it was supposed to be halfway through its hour-long lifespan, barely a quarter of it has gone.

As the two burning ends of the first rope were about to meet, Jack readied the unlit end of the second rope. He placed it in the fire the moment the first rope burned out. It caught light instantly.

"So we know there's thirty minutes left on this second rope if burning from just one end. Now both ends are lit it should burn twice as fast, in fifteen minutes."

"Yes, I know, we've been through this. Why are you telling me again like I'm daft," grumbled Cally.

"Er ... because I'm checking we've got it right. Because we have to eat the nut once it's cooked. Because we will die if we don't cook it for the correct amount of time. Need any other reasons?" Jack was getting wound up.

"All right, Sir Moodalot," scoffed Cally. "Calm down."

"How can I calm down when we're about to have to eat a deadly nut? **YOU** calm down."

"I don't need to. I'm not panicking like you," she retorted angrily.

"How can you be so confident when we're in such danger?"

Cally shrugged. **"I don't know. Maybe I don't care what happens to me any more."**

Jack found this answer unnerving but he didn't pursue it. There was a sadness to Cally, a deep sadness underneath all that bravado, and it frightened Jack a little.

"That rope is hardly burning," he said.

It wasn't. It had barely shortened since they had lit the second end.

The door burst open and Deuce and Bruce strolled in.

"Knock, knock," said Bruce.

"Who's there?" said Deuce.

"Boo."

"Boo who?"

"Boo hoo, you didn't cook the nut for the right amount of time and now you're dead!"

They chuckled and slapped each other on the back. Jeff Onions woke and stretched extravagantly.

"Wow. Lots of rope to go," said Bruce. "You sure you've got this right?"

"Yes," said Cally defiantly. **"Jack worked it out and I trust him."**

Jack found himself blushing. It had been a while since someone had thought he was worth listening to – he had got into the habit of letting his dad make all his decisions for him. He felt an impulse to say, "Please don't rely on me, I could easily be wrong," but the calculations he and Cally had come up with were right, he was sure of it. There was no doubt about it, though – there was loads of the second rope left. Too much.

"And old Jeff Onions here is pretty rude," said Cally. "For a dog."

"Our dog?" Deuce stared. **"You mean Bessie? I hate to break this to you, but dogs can't talk."**

"Well, this one did," said Jack. **"And he told us his name was Jeff Onions."**

Bruce and Deuce thought this was the funniest thing they had ever heard. They threw back their heads and roared with laughter.

"He did!" insisted Cally. **"Jeff, tell them."**

The dog stood up, tail wagging, ears up, and started to bark excitedly.

"Oh for goodness' sake," muttered Cally.

"Enough joking around," said Bruce. "We're getting hungry. Is it time for our nut yet?"

Cally and Jack looked at the rope. They were both thinking the same thing – it *did* feel like about fifteen minutes had passed since they had lit the final end, but the rope was still long. Had they miscalculated? What should they do?

"It's fine," said Cally. "Have patience. You'll get your nut."

"Whatever you say," said Bruce.

Cally whispered to Jack, "I think we should take it out now. There's loads of rope left!"

"Just wait," said Jack. "Have some faith. We mustn't guess, remember."

Trouble was, Jack was full of doubt too, but he felt they should stick to his plan. Cally had said she trusted him and he wanted so badly not to let her down.

Cally shook her head. "I've had enough of waiting." She reached for the rope.

"Wait!" said Jack. **"Look!"**

He pointed to the rope, which was suddenly disappearing at an incredible rate. It burned through nearly a quarter of its overall length in just a couple of seconds.

And it was gone.

"Wow!" said Cally. "That's so sneaky of it. Had me worried."

Jack grabbed the nut from its holder using a pair of iron tongs lying by the fire. He put it down on the table in front of Deuce and Bruce.

"Forty-five minutes. Exactly."

Deuce pulled a penknife out of his pocket and flicked out a blade.

"Hope so," said Bruce, eyes fixed on the nut.

Deuce sliced the nut into quarters with care and pushed two pieces towards Jack and Cally.

"Come on, then," said Cally. **"Let's get this over with."**

They reached down, picked up a piece of nut each and put it into their mouths.

The nut was indeed an experience like no other Jack had ever had. At first it tasted of, well, nut. But then it began. It started in his toes; a warm feeling gave way to heat that was almost uncomfortable. Like Jack had placed his feet into a too-hot bath.

Had they got it wrong? Were they dying?

Jack opened his mouth to speak, but no words came.

His whole body felt like it was beginning to soften and collapse, like a melting snowman. As if his bones were liquefying and his whole frame would momentarily slide to the floor.

A freezing bolt of electricity shot up his spine, a thin river of steel and ice in the warm pudding he had become, slamming into his head and exploding like a small star, showering sparks and sharp diamond glitter and frozen fire. Every nerve lit up, he felt himself convulse, arms and legs spasmed, his eyes opened wide and light flooded in: golden, honey, warming. He writhed with intense joy, his fingers stretched wide, and then it was over.

He burped.

"Any good?" asked Bruce.

"Tasty?" asked Deuce.

Jack couldn't speak.

"I've tasted better," said Cally. **"Now, how about that key?"**

The key slid into the lock and the door opened. On the other side, behind his desk, opening a pack of Rich Tea fingers, sat Gary.

"Gary. It's almost good to see you," said Cally.

"How did it go?" asked Gary.

"Well, we didn't die," said Jack. "But we're no closer to getting home. What was the point of all that?"

"You are making progress," said Gary, counting out biscuits and popping them into his mouth. "You wouldn't be getting through these rooms if you weren't making progress."

"I suppose Jack was quite impressive in there," Cally said.

"Oh," Jack gulped.

Gary was having great difficulty manoeuvring the fifteen biscuits around his mouth to chew them.

"Don't get cocky," Cally warned Jack.

"I wasn't."

Gary began to make a quiet choking noise.

"I'm glad I'm not doing this alone," said Jack.

"Oh, don't get all soppy on me!"

Then they noticed Gary's head hitting the table with a *thump*.

"Gary – are you all right?" asked Cally.

They raced around the desk and tried to pull him upright, but he was heavy. It wasn't easy.

He was making strange rasping noises.

"What should we do?!" yelled Cally, instantly

panicked. "Gary!! GARY!!! Stop it!"

"He can't stop it," said Jack gently. "Calm down."

"I CAN'T CALM DOWN HE MIGHT DIE PLEASE DON'T DIE GARY!" yelled Cally.

Cally grabbed Gary by the collar and started to shake him backwards and forwards. Gary's eyes were rolling back so that only the whites of his eyes were visible.

"OH NO!! OH NO!! OH NO!!!" screamed Cally.

"Please be quiet," said Jack, "and stop shaking him."

Cally let go of Gary's collar and started whacking him on the back as hard as she could.

"GARY!"

Thwack.

"BREATHE!"

Jack grabbed Cally by the wrists and looked her in the eye.

"Cally, you have to stop – get over there by the wall and stay there."

Cally was wild-eyed and taking in big gulps of air, but she did as he had asked.

Jack went behind Gary, put his arms around his stomach and stuck a thumb into his belly. He wrapped his other hand around that one and started jabbing his hands upwards into Gary's abdomen, just above the belly button.

Cally shouted, "Think of all the biscuits! You'll make him sick!"

"That …" said Jack.

Thrust.

"... is kind of ..."

Thrust.

"... the idea."

Thrust.

Gary looked up, purple-faced, opened his mouth wide, and out shot a large wet pellet of half-chewed Rich Tea fingers.

At the same moment the door opposite his desk opened, and Wanda walked in saying, **DAAAAAARRRRRRLINGS!** before she was hit square in the mouth by Gary's flying soggy mass of biscuit.

Gary coughed violently a couple of times and, laying his forehead back on the desk, took in several huge gulps of air.

Jack was breathing heavily after all his efforts.

Wanda stood bolt upright, looking extremely surprised, eyes swivelling from person to person in the room.

"Darlings," she said after a few moments. "What was that?"

Cally still wasn't recovered enough to speak so she simply pointed at Gary. Gary looked up and said,

"That, Wanda, was fifteen half-chewed Rich Tea fingers."

"I see," said Wanda carefully. "I see."

"You're welcome."

"Are you OK, Gary?" asked Jack.

"I'm OK," said Gary. "I'm quite hungry."

"Sorry I was so useless," said Cally, "I just panicked."

"You can say that again." Jack grinned. "You completely went to pieces!"

Jack felt pleased with himself. "I guess being a robot is quite handy sometimes."

"It's not funny," said Cally. **What if you hadn't been here? Gary would have died and it would have been my fault."**

"Well, it would partly have been Gary's fault. He did ram half a packet of biscuits into his mush in one go."

"Fair enough," said Gary, "but I was quite peckish."

"Maybe," said Cally, "but, you know, you always wonder how you'll cope if there's a crisis. Will you rise to the occasion and be a hero or will you go to pieces and be a waste of space? Turns out, I'm a waste of space."

"Stop feeling sorry for yourself," said Jack. "I was glad you were here."

"Were you?"

"Yes. And the fact you panicked so much makes me think you care more than you let on."

"Whatever."

"Wanda's the one I feel for. Swallowing half a packet of half-chewed biscuits. **Yuk!**"

"What doesn't kill me will make me stronger," Wanda said stoically. She smoothed her clothes, cracked the knuckles on her fingers and coughed lightly. Then she smiled her biggest smile.

"Ya wanna take a trip?" she screeched.

"What's that accent you're doing?" Cally asked.

"Ooh uh dunnoo," said Wanda. **"Ah'm tryin'**

it ooon fer size. Ya liiiike?"

"Yes," said Jack.

"No," said Cally. "It makes you sound like a sleepy American crossed with a confused Australian crossed with a Cornish sailor."

"That sounds like my kind of party!!" said Wanda, gracefully sliding her feet apart until she was doing the splits.

"Do we have to go somewhere?" asked Cally.

"No, you can stay here. You want to stay here?"

Cally and Jack looked at Gary, who was slowly reaching into the top drawer of the desk and taking out a party bag of ginger nuts.

"No," said Cally. "But we also don't want to keep going into different rooms and then coming back again. We want to go home. Can't you help us, Wanda? Give us some sort of clue?"

"Listen, my pair of little Hot Patooties, you gotta figure this out for yourselves. I'm here to help, but I can't do this for you. You've gotta do it yourselves."

"But do *what*?" Cally wailed.

"You have to pay attention," said Wanda simply. "Work with what you're given. Get from room to room. Some things are within your power to influence, others are not. You need to work out which is which."

"How can we work out what to do if we don't know where we're trying to get to?" said Cally at last.

"Exactly," said Wanda—unhelpfully,

thought Jack.

They stood quietly for a moment.

"Here's what I *can* tell you," said Wanda. "And you might want to listen up too, Gary."

Gary was rooting through a cardboard box that had "Various Biscuits" written on the side.

"There's a difference," continued Wanda, **"between what you want and what you need."**

"Right," said Cally. "Well, I *want* to go home and I *need* to go home. So … I should go home."

"I'll leave that with you," continued Wanda.

Gary shoved fourteen ginger nuts into his mouth.

"Should we keep going?" asked Cally.

"Oh, always keep going. That's how things become clearer. And listen carefully – there are no shortcuts. Understand? Don't try to

take any shortcuts, you'll cause yourselves more problems in the long run."

Jack sighed. "I want to see my dad," he said. "Even if it's just for a minute. He'll be really worried about me."

Wanda, from her position on the floor in the splits, remained impassive.

"Look," said Wanda, "I'm doing the splits!" She grimaced. "Not sure I can get up though. Gary, put down those biscuits and give me a hand," she ordered. "And you two, off you go! Through the door; clap your hands to turn the light on. **Don't move until you have!**"

They went through the door, which slammed behind them. On the other side was total darkness. Jack clapped his hands, but nothing happened.

"What is wrong with them all?" said Cally angrily. "They're messing with our heads. Why is it so dark?"

"I don't know," said Jack quietly. "But I think Wanda is on our side."

"Is she though? If she's on our side, why are we in an empty dark room? Why doesn't she help us get home?"

"Quite windy, isn't it?" noticed Jack.

Cally clapped her hands but, again, nothing happened.

"I'm going to try and find a light switch," she said.

"No! Wanda said don't move until the light comes on!"

"But it isn't coming on."

Cally tried clapping again. Nothing.

"It is quite windy, you're right. Think

someone left the window open?"

"I might go back and ask her about the light," suggested Jack, feeling for the door handle behind him. But there was nothing there.

"The door's gone."

They both clapped their hands together furiously. No light.

"Wait," said Cally. "They want us to work together, right? We got through the last room by working together."

"Good idea," said Jack, holding up one of his palms. **"Give me five."**

"I can't see you."

"I'm right here. Ow!"

"Oh sorry, was that not your hand?"

"That was my face."

"Well, it's really dark!"

"Try again."

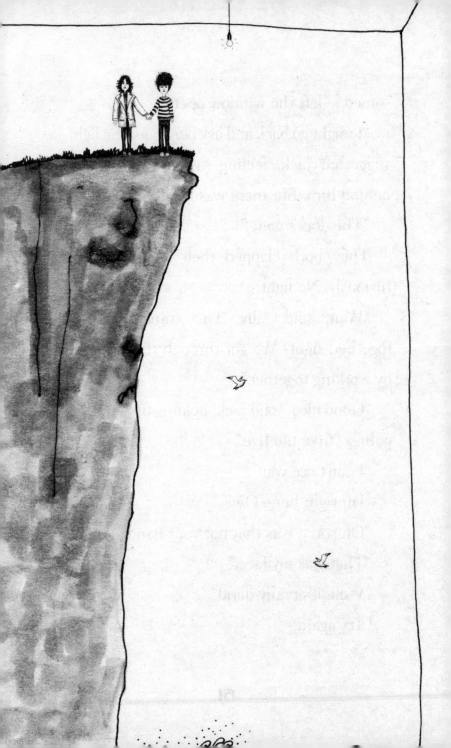

Cally swung and this time connected with Jack's hand.

The lights came on.

They were in another room. Above them was a ceiling, much like the ceilings in all the other rooms. To their left was a white wall. To their right was another white wall.

And, in front of them, the edge of a cliff.

They were standing on the top of a cliff.

A cliff so high it was hard to see what lay at the bottom of it and, frankly, it was too scary to look down and find out. Jack thought he could hear the sea crashing against rocks. Their toes were sticking out over the edge.

Instinctively they reached out for each other's hands and held on tight, then took a cautious step backwards.

This was still a room, Jack thought, a

room with a huge cliff, grass underfoot and, apparently, some sea down there somewhere.

"For God, Queen and country!" shouted someone behind them.

Cally and Jack turned, quickly but carefully.

Facing them was a group of about thirty animals.

Several horses, one zebra, a sheep, two ostriches, several small rodenty creatures, half a dozen dogs, an elephant, two white tigers, a polar bear and a flamingo.

The animals were wearing clothes. In fact, they were dressed very smartly. The zebra was wearing a blue blazer with a cravat under a crisp checked shirt. The elephant wore a huge dress with a floral pattern, the horses all had tidy, brushed or pleated manes; a couple of them wore fedoras. It was as if, thought Jack, animals from a zoo had been dressed up to attend a garden party. They were all smiling. But despite the smiles and the smart clothes, Jack felt uneasy. He was conscious of the sheer physical size and strength of these animals, blazers or not. The hairs stood up on the back of his neck.

The animals were uncomfortably close and he wanted to move away, but he couldn't. He was fully aware of the huge drop behind him.

"For God, Queen and country!" they shouted again.

A frog-faced, rotund little green creature elbowed its way to the front of the group.

"But not necessarily in that order!" he boomed at Jack and Cally. He threw his head back and roared with laughter, his whole face contorting in violent pleasure at his own joke. It provoked much mirth in the rest of the group

too and they cackled along with him, mouths open wide, paws on stomachs, bodies shaking with pleasure.

Jack smiled politely, mainly out of fear. Cally didn't.

"The name's Maverick," the frog-faced creature bellowed. "I didn't choose it, they did! Apparently, I'm a bit of a ruddy rebel!"

He was dressed, Jack thought, exactly how he imagined Toad of Toad Hall might have dressed – tweed suit, waistcoat, brown shoes. In fact, Jack wondered if this *was* Toad.

"A webel and a wuddy legend!" said a pony in a dress.

"Your words, not mine, Martha!" They all chuckled heartily at this.

"Are you Toad?" Jack found himself asking. **"You know, of Toad Hall?"**

There was suddenly a noticeable tension in the group. The flamingo's eyes widened. Below him Jack could hear distant waves crashing against rocks.

Maverick's eyes narrowed. "Do I look like a toad?" he said quietly.

"Um. . ."

"Have I got short, stumpy legs? Is my skin rough and thick?"

"Well. . ."

"No, they aren't. No, it isn't. My skin is beautifully smooth and covered in delicious mucus, is it not? My legs are slender and shapely, are they not? Yes, they are. A toad?! How dare you! I am a pure-bred frog. I come from a long and glorious line of frogs. Are you

seriously trying to tell me that you can't tell the difference between a frog and a toad?"

"Not really," stammered Jack. "Sorry. My mistake."

"Does it matter?" Cally interrupted.

"DOES IT MATTER?!" screamed Maverick. "Of course it matters! I wouldn't cross the road to help a toad, but I would die for a fellow frog!"

"Die!" yelled a highly manicured and breathtakingly ugly little hairless rodent squatting to Maverick's left.

"Quiet, Yaxley!" ordered Maverick.

"Yes, sir, sorry, sir," yipped Yaxley in a high-pitched voice.

"Allow us to introduce ourselves," said Maverick smoothly, smiling again. "We are the Creatures of Ham: we are the

right-minded, the fair, the balanced, the civilized. We are the indigenous creatures of this region."

"This region?" asked Jack. "Do you mean this room?"

"Who are you?" Maverick asked, ignoring Jack's question.

"No – who are *you*?" retorted Cally.

"Who am I?" barked Maverick.

"Who is he?" screeched Yaxley.

"Stand down, Eggs Mayhem!" boomed Maverick.

"Eggs Mayhem?" asked Cally.

"That's my secret code name!" Yaxley boasted.

"Not so secret now," pointed out Cally.

Maverick threw her a dark look and said,

"Read your book, Yaxley!"

"Yes, sir, sorry, sir," whimpered Yaxley. He whipped out a serious-looking hardback book and began to read. Jack could see the book was upside down but thought better of pointing that out.

"I shall tell you who I am. My full title," continued Maverick, "**is Lord of all the Beasts of the Earth and Fishes of the Sea**. I'm frightened of cats, I invented the hamburger, I write poems about bread, I dress up as a cowboy in my spare time, I wear silky pants, I collect wristbands, I have two pet cows, I only eat mashed potato and clear soup because I'm very farty, and if my food is not served in my giraffe bowl I throw it on to the floor and kick it as far away as possible."

"Quite right," squeaked Yaxley.

"I was the Leapfrog Champion of my

village when I was eleven, I outlawed Scrabble because it's too intellectual, I love Disney films, especially *Snow White and the Seven Dwarves*, I eat my own bogeys because they are packed with nutrition, I am the Voodoo Spirit of Death, and I've banned beards."

"Stupid beards," said Yaxley, punching himself in the jaw.

"I really, really want a house with a gold lift in it and I've expelled all pandas from round here because, you know, why not? Think that just about covers it."

"My turn! My turn!" pleaded Yaxley, jumping up and down with one of his feet as high in the air as he could manage. **"Pick me! Pick me!"**

"OK, Yaxley," Maverick said in the tone of a weary parent talking to a toddler. "Tell us about you."

"I'm a naked mole-rat," said Yaxley proudly. **"I'm a victim and I'm superior."**

There was a pause. Yaxley seemed to be trying very hard to think of something else to say but nothing was forthcoming. He stared at the ground with his mouth open.

"So, you are welcome to our region," said Maverick after a while, wiggling his froggy eyebrows. "But you should know that we have a certain way of doing things, a way that things have always been done. If you came here to cause trouble, well, we won't have it. Nobody likes a troublemaker. We have a civilized, calm, polite, *fair* way of doing things here and you are welcome to participate so long as you know your place and behave accordingly."

"How lovely," said Cally. "And what happens

if we refuse to follow this 'code of behaviour'?"

"Slavery or death!" chanted Yaxley, doing a little jig.

"He's kidding!" said Maverick.

"No, I'm not! You said earlier, it's slavery or death!" said Yaxley.

"Hendo. . ." said Maverick with a meaningful look to a big horse at the back.

Hendo trotted sharply over to Yaxley, picked him up by the scruff of his neck like a kitten, and carried him out of the way to the back of the group.

"Oh no! Oh no!" screamed Yaxley, his little hairless pink legs kicking the air as he dangled. "I told you I was a victim! But I'm still superior!"

Maverick opened his mouth to speak, then stopped and looked around at the animals. He wrinkled his nose.

"Wait," he said. "Did one of you. . .? **OK, who did that?**"

The group parted, leaving the sheep standing meekly alone. It had a pile of pellets underneath it.

"For goodness' sake, Gertie!" said Maverick. "I'm trying to make a good impression on. . ."

"Cally and Jack," said Cally.

"On Cally here. Couldn't you have waited? I've a good mind to let Hortensia eat you, Gertie."

One of the tigers lifted its head.

"Oooh, yes please!" said Hortensia, stretching extravagantly.

"Behave yourselves, all of you," warned Maverick, turning back to Cally and Jack.

"How do we get the key, please?" asked Jack. He didn't like the way the flamingo was looking at him.

"Ah, yes," said Maverick. "The key."

He motioned to the polar bear.

"Young gentleman here wants the key, Gregory."

The polar bear ambled over to Jack. He towered over him.

"Wow," spluttered Jack. "You're big. I, um, like your sweater. Burgundy suits you. Do you find it hard to get clothes in your size?"

"Humankind's only natural predator, the polar bear," grinned Maverick. "Astonishingly strong and epically stupid. I love the stupid."

Gregory held out his closed paw. It was bigger than Jack's head. Slowly, he unfurled his enormous furry toes, each one tipped with a thick, sharp claw. His paw was empty.

"Er," said Jack, trying to sound cheerful. **"I wanted a key!"**

"*I wanted a key*?" mocked Maverick. "Who do you think you are? If you want a key, you have to earn it! You don't get something for nothing, you know. **You are a very spoilt boy.**"

Maverick turned to Cally.

"I bet *you* don't always get everything you ask for, do you, Cally?"

"No I don't, but. . ." she began.

"Exactly!" said Maverick. "The rest of us, honest, hard-working, ordinary creatures, have to earn our privileges, but it seems the rules simply don't apply to Jack here. He thinks he's special. He thinks he's different. Well, I'm afraid your days of free handouts are over."

Jack said nothing. Partly because he couldn't

get a word in edgeways. And partly because a polar bear twice his height was looming over him.

Maverick beckoned to Cally and drew her aside. Jack could still hear him though, because Maverick had such a booming voice.

"You see," Maverick said to Cally, "we have your key. And you need that key, don't you, um. . ."

"Cally."

"Cally. I see how strong and clever you are, Cally. I admire you. You seem to possess a strength and intelligence that, if I may say so, I don't see in your friend. Are you finding him a burden?"

"Not particularly. . ." she began.

"Yes, I thought so." He sighed noisily. "There have been times when he's let you down. If it

169

wasn't for him, you would be out of here by now. You'd be back home."

"What are you suggesting? You want me to drop Jack?" asked Cally.

"Drop him! Why didn't I think of that? Drop him off the cliff!! What a brilliant idea!"

"No, wait, I didn't. . ." began Cally, but Maverick was already hopping back to the group.

"Cally suggests we drop Jack off the cliff! Gregory!"

At this, Gregory the polar bear grabbed Jack by the shoulders and swung him out over the yawning chasm. Jack felt a salty breeze from below buffet him. He wondered why it was so much windier now he was suspended over the drop. Then he looked down at the fall beneath him and forgot all about the wind. It was a sheer drop, a long way down, he thought, on to rocks and waves.

Jack screamed.

"I didn't mean that!" she insisted.

"It was your idea, Cally!"

Jack stopped screaming. He was worried the bear would drop him if he was too much trouble. So he hung there stiffly.

"Cally," continued Maverick, "Jack knows exactly how to get out of the Rooms. He's had help all along. He's just not sharing it with you."

"What?!" spluttered Cally.

"Didn't you know that, Cally? It's well

known, isn't it, everyone?"

The animals all nodded.

"I don't believe you," Cally said.

"I'm sorry to have to be the one to break it to you," said Maverick.

"What are you talking about?" demanded Cally.

"Has he solved puzzles since he's been in here? Difficult puzzles?"

"Yes."

"There you go. You think he did that on his own without help? Oh please. Watch, he'll deny it."

Maverick turned to Jack. "Jack, have you had secret help in here?"

"No!"

"See?" said Maverick to Cally. He turned back to Jack. "Have you been told the secret to getting out?"

"No!" pleaded Jack. **"That's not true! None of that is true!"**

"Aha!" shouted Maverick triumphantly. "Didn't I tell you he'd deny it!"

"Exactly!" hissed the flamingo. "You called it, Maverick."

"And you, Cally." Maverick leaned in close. "Have you been let in on these secrets? Have you been given special help?"

"No," said Cally, looking first to Maverick and then to Jack. **"No I haven't."**

"Is this the first time you've even heard about it?"

Cally nodded.

"I can't say I'm surprised," said Maverick in a sad voice. "They treat us with such contempt."

He turned to Jack.

"Let's see if we can get you to be straight with us. Let's see if we can get you to tell the truth for once. Say 'I'm Jack'," instructed Maverick.

"I'm Jack," said Jack immediately. He didn't need to be asked twice.

"Say 'I have kept things from Cally'," said Maverick.

"But that's not true."

"Just tell us you have had secret help – stop wasting our time," bellowed Maverick.

Jack looked helplessly at Cally.

"I..." he began.

"JUST SAY IT!" screamed Maverick.

Jack could feel Gregory loosen his grip.

"I've had help!" blurted Jack. **"Please, please!"**

Gregory gripped him tightly again.

There was a silence. All eyes were on Cally.

"I . . . he was going to drop me and. . ." Jack didn't know what to say.

"I think the time for talking is over," said Maverick. "You're angry, Cally, and I don't blame you. I think the time for standing by and doing nothing is over. We must take back control. Shall we drop him, Cally?"

"Will you give me the key if we do?" she said.

"Yes, I'll give *you* the key," said Maverick. "Once we drop him."

Cally frowned. "Why isn't there a puzzle? There's usually a puzzle."

"This is the puzzle, Cally. You're just smart enough to have figured it out. **Drop him and you'll get your key.** "

Cally looked to Jack.

"You put me in a difficult position, Maverick," she said. "I really do want that key."

"Of course you do," oozed Maverick.

"And you're right. I haven't really known Jack for very long so I don't know for sure if I can trust him."

"You can't," said Maverick firmly.

Cally chewed on her lip as she looked at Jack dangling from the polar bear's grip.

"So it is tempting," she said, "to just let him fall. But there's something I've noticed that makes me stop and think."

"Think?" scoffed Maverick. "Wouldn't waste your time doing too much of that, girlie."

"I was thinking," Cally continued, "That you animals ... well maybe not *you*, Maverick ... but your pals, some of them are very strong indeed. They could tear us limb from limb in moments. So ... why don't they? Why mess around with trying to have me make the decision to throw Jack off a cliff? They could just eat him if they wanted to."

"Because we are civilized," explained Maverick.

"So you keep saying. My gran used to say that if someone repeatedly tells you what they are like, they're usually the exact opposite."

"Your gran sounds like a barrel of laughs. Are you going to join us or not?"

"For instance, my cousin Annabel. She used to tell us she was as **'mad as a box of frogs'**."

"I object to that expression," sniffed Maverick.

"Fair enough," said Cally. "She'd tell us it all the time. Gran said Annabel really said that because inside she was scared that she was actually quite boring."

"Well this is all very fascinating, but..."

"And my great-grandfather told everyone that feelings were for wimps. Gran said it was actually because he felt everything so deeply, he thought he'd struggle to cope if he gave in to those feelings." Cally shrugged. "Gran said if someone tells you over and over how happy they are, it's likely they're really quite sad. Or if they tell you that you can trust them more than anyone else in the whole wide world, then you probably can't trust them at all. And you, Maverick, you keep telling me how *civilized* you are. Which makes me think that you're the exact opposite."

Maverick put his hands in his pockets. **"Oh dear. How disappointing you are turning out to be. And how stupid."**

"That story you told me, about how Jack's been getting secret help – that could be true. But why tell me? You could have chucked Jack over the cliff in a second. It's almost like you want us to turn us against each other."

"Now listen to me—" Maverick began.

"I haven't finished yet," said Cally, her voice cold. Jack realized she was very angry, but for once she wasn't shouting. She was a laser beam of quiet, pure rage. She lowered her voice so the other animals, who were standing further off, couldn't hear her, but Jack was just close enough to make out what she was saying.

"So why? That's the question. Why make me kill Jack when you could just do it? Because you need *them*," she nodded to the animals, "to believe it's all civilized and reasonable. That's your story, isn't it? The story you hide behind, the one you sell to your supporters. If you blackmail me into betraying Jack, then you'll be able to kill him. You'll get to satisfy your longing for destruction and chaos and violence, and you'll feel powerful. You *would* be powerful. But you have to take your supporters along with you. And so you dress it up as a reasonable, moral crusade even though you don't believe a word. You make up a load of rubbish about a hidden enemy that, conveniently, no one can see. You make up an enemy to electrify your followers, unify them behind you with resentment and fear. Those animals with you" – Cally gestured to the group of animals looking over at them – "I'm sure some of them think exactly the way you do: Yaxley, that polar bear. But Gertie the sheep, that elephant, the dogs – you need them, you need the muscle, you need the numbers, but they don't really think like you so you have to make sure you keep them on board. So you lie to them."

"You're calling me a liar, Cally?" spat back Maverick, his slimy green throat sac bulging. **"Have you told Jack the whole truth?"**

"The only thing that matters," said Cally, ignoring him, "is that Jack and I are a team. We are in this together. I'm not leaving without him. So if you want to throw him off the cliff, I can't stop you. But if you do, I'm jumping off after him. Because Jack is my friend."

Cally turned to the group. "I've made my decision. I don't want Jack to be thrown over the cliff. And if you throw him over, I'm jumping off with him."

"What?!" Maverick began in his loud voice, but Cally cut him off.

"You see, everyone, I was just telling Maverick how poor Jack here has lost his mother recently."

The group all turned to Jack.

"She was a wonderful woman. Kind, loving, incredibly committed to Jack. A terrible loss. And I was telling Maverick about my grandmother, who also died recently. She. . ."

Cally stopped for a second.

Jack saw Maverick opening his mouth to

speak so he said quickly, **"Take your time, Cally, take your time. No one will interrupt you; we're all listening."** Maverick glared at Jack but said nothing.

Gertie the sheep, Jack noticed, had tears in her eyes.

Cally continued.

"She was the most important person in my life and now she is dead, and I am in bits. Like Jack. Two children, grieving, alone and vulnerable. All we want to do is go home. Maverick, as you know, has the key that we need." She smiled. **"And he has offered it to us. No conditions."**

Yaxley couldn't contain himself.

"What?!?!?" he shrieked. Hortense the tiger, also clearly surprised and unhappy with the way this was going, nevertheless placed a paw heavily on Yaxley's shoulder to shut him up. The other animals, though, looked deeply moved.

"That's all very sad, we sympathize with you enormously..." began Maverick. **"But I'm afraid that won't be possible."**

Cally ran towards the edge of the cliff and with a huge leap she jumped out over the edge, high into the air, towards Jack. For a moment she was suspended in mid-air, out over empty space, certain death below, until she landed heavily on to Jack, throwing her arms around his shoulders and neck and clinging on for dear life.

The animals gasped.

The flamingo screamed.

Gertie fainted.

The zebra couldn't look.

The elephant shouted, **"No!"**

Cally's leap on to Jack so took Gregory by surprise that he nearly dropped them both, the extra weight of Cally making the bear stagger. But he regained his balance and held Jack and Cally steadily over the drop. Cally hung there with her arms around Jack's neck.

"We are in this together!" shouted Cally again.

Jack was delighted she was with him and on his side, but he wasn't sure this was the best idea she'd ever had.

Maverick called out, **"Bring them in, Gregory, bring them in. Goodness me! What a fuss!"**

Gregory, who was getting a little tired holding Jack, and now Cally, brought them back over solid ground and lowered them to the floor.

"You passed the test!" shouted Martha, the pony, delightedly.

"We did?" asked Cally.

"Yes! I'm so pleased!"

"Yes, we're so pleased," repeated Maverick unconvincingly. He looked furious. **"Decency wins! Here's the key."**

"Thank you, sir. And thank you all," said Cally, taking the key. "Which way is the door, please?"

A golden retriever led them to a small red door hidden behind a bush.

The door closed behind them and Cally and Jack found themselves in the dark.

"Turn the light on please, Gary," Jack called out.

There was no response.

"Cally," said Jack after a moment. "All that stuff about secret help ... I don't know anything about it, I promise."

Cally shook her head scornfully. "That was all made up."

"Thanks for sticking with me," Jack said. **"And ... I'm sorry about your gran."**

Even in the dark, he could tell that Cally was glaring at him. **"You see!"** she snapped. "That is exactly why I don't like telling people things!

They become so annoying! I don't want to talk about her. Or think about her. You'd better not mention her again or we are *through*. Gary, for goodness' sake, are you there?" she shouted. **"Turn the light on!"**

She stopped. The room was filling with what seemed to be fog. They became aware of eerie music playing very quietly, perhaps an organ. They heard the sound of distant laughter but could see nothing in the darkness.

Jack felt along the wall by the door for a light switch.

"DARE YOU ENTER," said a deep booming voice that made them both jump. **"DARE YOU ENTER THE HOUSE OF MASSIVE TERROR?!"**

Jack and Cally froze.

"DO YOU?" came the voice again. **"DO YOU DARE? DARE YOU DO? DO YOU?"**

Jack peered into the gloom, but could see nothing.

"YOU ARE TOO SCARED!!! HOW SAD," the deep voice continued. **"I PITY YOU, MORTALS."**

Jack felt along the wall on the other side of the door.

"YOU ARE SMALL. YOU ARE WEAK. YOU ARE NOTHING."

Jack found a light switch.

"I, THOUGH, AM MIGHTY. I AM STRONG. I AM IMMORTAL."

Jack flicked the switch. A fluorescent light on the ceiling came on, but there was so much smoke it was hard to see anything.

"HEY! TURN THE LIGHT OFF!" said the voice, still deep and booming but suddenly sounding concerned.

Jack and Cally took a couple of steps further

into the room.

"Wait! This is not Gary's office!" said Cally excitedly.

"That's not good though, is it?" said Jack.

"It's great! It means we're getting somewhere!"

"It does?"

"Yes, we've ended up back in his office each time, but this is somewhere new! This has got to be progress!"

"I MEAN IT," said the voice. **"SERIOUSLY. TURN THE LIGHT OFF!"**

As Jack and Cally edged carefully forwards through the murky haze, they became aware of a small sofa facing a sheet suspended from the ceiling. Wires ran along the floor from the walls to behind the sheet.

"I ADVISE YOU TO TURN BACK. YOU ARE IN GRAVE DANGER."

"That's a scary voice," said Cally.

"Let me deal with this," said Jack, as confidently as he could.

"GRAVE DANGER! GRAVE–"

Jack stepped forward and pulled back the sheet.

Sitting at a small table, speaking into a microphone, was a thin boy of about twelve. On the desk was a nameplate that read **"DWAIN PIPE"**.

There was a pause as the boy looked at them and they looked at him.

"PLEASE TAKE A SEAT," Dwain said into the microphone, his words booming out from speakers behind him. **"ON THE SOFA."** He turned off the microphone.

"Please," Dwain said politely. "Please do take a seat."

DWAIN PIPE

Jack and Cally sat down.

"Now, then, let's get started," said the boy. He was dressed in a three-piece suit with a neat side-parting. **"Would you rather have toes for fingers or fingers for toes?"**

"Excuse me?" said Jack.

"Would you," said Dwain calmly, **"rather have toes where your fingers are supposed to be or fingers where your toes are supposed to be?"**

"Leave this to me," said Jack confidently. Cally shrugged.

Jack leaned forward and placed his elbows on to the desk.

"It's great to meet you, Dwain."

"I need an answer please."

"My name is Jack, this is Cally. We'd love to chat, but we do need the key. Could you please give it to us and we'll be on our way?"

Dwain didn't blink. "I need an answer please," he said again.

"Of course we could answer your riddle, but you could just save us all a lot of time and give us the—"

"Time's up," Dwain said matter-of-factly, punching a button on the keyboard in front of him.

Simultaneously Jack and Cally let out a cry of pain and both began to frantically pull at their shoes and socks. They couldn't get them off their feet quick enough.

They looked down at their feet in horror.

Within moments their big toes were thumbs, the rest of the toes fingers.

"What the..." began Jack.

A peculiar sensation pulsed through their hands and they watched as their fingers shrank and became toes.

Cally held her hands up in astonishment.

"What have you done?" she gasped.

"No decision results in both options activating," stated Dwain. "I did say I needed an answer."

Jack was too busy staring aghast at his hands to respond.

Dwain reached into a cabinet behind him and pulled out a tray with four glasses containing liquid. He put two in front of Jack and two in front of Cally.

"Would you rather drink tiger wee or gorilla spit?"

"You what?" Cally said, turning white.

gorilla spit

tiger wee

gorilla spit

more tiger wee

"Would you rather drink tiger wee or gorilla spit?"

"Why?" asked Jack, eyeing the glasses in front of him. One indeed could well have been urine; it had a greeny-yellow hue. The other liquid could just as easily have been spit; it was frothy and bubbly.

"Would you rather drink tiger wee or gorilla spit?" Dwain said calmly. "I need an answer please. No decision results in—"

"Spit!" shouted Cally. "Gorilla spit."

"Really?" said Jack with disgust. "You'd drink spit that came from a gorilla's mouth?!"

"It's better than drinking wee from a tiger!"

"Good point but … OK, spit!"

"Thank you," said Dwain, removing the

glasses containing the greeny-yellow liquids from in front of them and placing them back in the cabinet.

He turned and looked expectantly at them and then at the remaining glasses.

"You're kidding," said Jack. **"No way!"**

Dwain raised an eyebrow and that was enough for Jack. The kid had a powerful presence and it didn't seem wise to deny him again.

Reaching forward, Jack tried to pick up the glass with one hand but his toe-fingers made that virtually impossible. It was like trying to pick up a glass with, well, a foot.

Using both hands and holding the glass between his palms, Jack picked it up and put it to his lips. Without giving himself time to think about what he was doing he threw back the frothy viscous liquid in one go. The glass was only about a quarter full but there was still plenty of spittle in it.

Cally looked at Jack, appalled.

Jack hammered his hands on the desk and threw himself bodily from side to side, squirming and writhing.

"That actually doesn't taste like what you think it's going to taste like," he said when finished.

Encouraged, Cally picked up her glass and threw the contents down her throat.

"It tastes way worse," continued Jack.

Cally swallowed it all in one go, retched a couple of times, screwed her face up as tightly as she could, dropped to her knees and let out a loud, piercing scream.

"Yes," said the boy. "Surprisingly, the tiger

wee actually has a more pleasant taste. Who would guess?"

"Why didn't you tell us that?" said Cally from the floor. "That gorilla spit was the most evil-tasting thing I've ever come across."

"It was like petrol, bad breath, the bottom of an old bin, battery acid and off-milk all mixed together," said Jack.

"That's quite a good description," said Cally. "**Rancid**. Now, Dwain, can you please put our feet and hands back the way they were, give us our key and we'll be on our way?"

"Would you rather have a bottom that shouted 'Ouch!' really loudly every time you sat down, or a hand that said, 'I smell!' quietly every time you touched anything?" said Dwain.

"**Oh no! No, no, no, no, no!**" responded Cally. "We did it, we drank the spit!"

"Would you rather have a bottom that shouted 'Ouch!' really loudly every time you sat down, or a hand that said, 'I smell!' quietly every time you touched anything?" repeated the boy.

"I'm going with my bottom shouting 'ouch', please," said Jack. "I'll just try and sit down less. Thanks very much."

"Thanks very much?" said Cally. "Why are you being so nice to him? I'm going with my hands saying 'I smell'. At least it'll be quiet."

"The 'ouch' for you," said the boy to Jack, tapping his keyboard. "The 'I smell' for you, Cally."

Cally reached up to the desk to pull herself up from the floor.

"I smell," said a faint, delicate voice from her left hand. **"I SMELL,"** said a deeper, bass voice from her right.

Jack hesitated, then lifted his bottom a little way off the sofa and sat back down again.

"Ouch!" it yelled, loudly.

"That's way louder than I was expecting!" said Jack. "How can I go into the cinema now or a restaurant or . . . anywhere?"

"We should be so lucky," said Cally. "I just want to get to the next room. Are we finished? Can we have our key, please?"

"Who's being polite now?" muttered Jack.

"Would you rather—" said Dwain.

OUCH!

"No! Please! We just want to go home," interrupted Cally.

"Would you rather," repeated Dwain, "be able to fly or be able to turn invisible?"

"Wow! That's two good ones," said Cally. She narrowed her eyes. "What's the catch?"

"*Are* they both good?" questioned Jack.

"Of course. Imagine being able to fly! Soaring over a city, swooping down anywhere that looks interesting. You'd be free to go anywhere you want, no walls could hold you, nothing could stop you."

"But everyone would find out about you. The amazing flying human. No privacy. You'd probably be captured and examined by scientists..."

"OK, fine," said Cally. "Then choose being invisible. You could go anywhere unnoticed, hear stuff you are not supposed to hear, spy on anyone – the Queen, the Prime Minister, anyone! No one would even know you were there."

Jack shrugged. **"I kind of already know what that's like,"** he said quietly.

"What do you mean?" asked Cally.

"I already know what being invisible feels like. I thought it would be easier, you see, if I made myself invisible. I needed to do it for a while; I couldn't face the world. But actually, if you do it for long enough, people stop seeing you. At school, no one talks to me. My dad doesn't listen to me. I've had enough of being invisible. I've had enough of looking on while other people do stuff."

Dwain looked at them both. "So what is your answer?"

"I smell," said Cally's left hand as she scratched her ear.

"I reject both," said Jack. "You can decide, Dwain."

"Ouch," shouted Jack's bottom as he shifted in his seat.

"You have to pick one," said Dwain.

"Then we both choose to fly," said Cally. "We don't have to use it now, Jack. But one day we might feel differently to how we do right now. We might want to fly. Let's pick that. Let's have that up our sleeve. What do you think? We don't have to use it but we'll always know it's there."

Jack shrugged.

"Right, both of you can fly," said Dwain. "Here's your key."

"That's it?" asked Cally.

"That's it," said Dwain. "There's the door."

Cally reached over to pick up the key.

"I smell, I smell, I smell, I smell, I smell, I smell, I smell..." said her right hand as she repeatedly tried and failed to pick the key up with her clumsy toe-fingers.

Jack picked the key up with his finger-toes, put it in his mouth, then walked over to the door where he sat down – "Ouch" – and put it in the lock.

Cally helped him to his feet – "I smell, I smell" – as they both walked through the door.

They forgot to say goodbye to Dwain Pipe, who signed a mournful sigh, switched on his microphone and said, **"ALONE AGAIN."**

The next room was tiny, no bigger than the inside of a small wardrobe, and seemed to have no ceiling. They both somehow squeezed in.

"It's like standing in a chimney," Cally said.

"Ouch," said Jack's bottom, as it pressed up against the wall.

"There's nothing in here," said Cally. "Where can they have hidden the key?"

"Press the walls, there might be a secret panel," suggested Jack.

"You're kidding?" said Cally.

"Why not?"

Cally sighed and began pushing the bits of wall around her.

"I smell, I smell, I smell, I smell," murmured her hands.

"Happy now?" she said.

"It is quite funny," laughed Jack.

Without warning, out from under the bottom of the walls scurried a swarm of insects, scores of them, black and fast. Hard, shiny bodies, long hairy legs, vibrating antennae.

Jack shrieked.

The insects raced up Cally's and Jack's legs, over their clothes, on to their arms, their hair. Some found their way into Cally's mouth and ears, on to Jack's neck, across his eyes, biting, scratching.

Jack and Cally thrashed about, trying desperately to brush them off, but there was so little space in the room it was virtually impossible. And still the creatures swarmed in.

Jack tried to open the door. Locked.

He closed his eyes, held his breath, tried to find some space in the chaos to think. He could feel insects crawling into his ears.

He looked up and opened his eyes. No ceiling.

Surely not? he thought.

"Shall we try crrhhhggaaafartttts?" he

spluttered.

"What?!" screamed Cally, frantically brushing insects from her face.

"Sorry, swallowed an insect," said Jack, retching slightly. "Shall we try flying?"

"We don't have any wings!" said Cally.

"True," said Jack.

Insects were crawling under his shirt; he could feel their little legs scurrying across his chest.

"I'm going to fly," he said to himself. He felt sure Dwain wouldn't have lied to them.

"I'm going to fly," he said again. And he did.

Jack shot upwards, leaving Cally staring in astonishment.

Jack wasn't great at flying. He couldn't control his direction very well and he careered from one side of the room to the other, slamming into the walls as he rose higher.

The insects, to Jack's great relief, began to pop, just like soap bubbles bursting. With tiny snapping noises, one by one, soon they were all gone.

Jack looked down and saw that Cally was arrowing towards him, a huge smile on her face.

Jack shot out of the top of the room and found himself high, high, high over beautiful countryside, blue skies above, warm sunshine. It was glorious.

Cally caught up with him and together they looped and spun through the clear sky, laughing with joy.

"We can fly!" shouted Jack. "I have no idea how I'm doing this."

"Who cares? We're doing it! And look − the key!"

Cally pointed and Jack saw that a

few feet away, suspended in the air, motionless, was a large key.

Cally flew over and hovered next to it and Jack, not yet having fully mastered the finer points of flying control, smashed into her. They both roared with laughter.

"I love this room!" he said. "Now we're up here and those insects are gone."

"Isn't this brilliant!" agreed Cally. "Aren't you glad we chose flying?"

"I think we've cracked it!" Jack said gleefully. **"I think we've escaped the Rooms at last!"**

He reached out, grabbed the key and everything changed.

The sky darkened, the temperature dropped and Cally and Jack fell out of the sky.

Both screamed.

They fell only a short distance before they landed, side by side, square on the back of a ten-foot-long giant duck, which flapped its enormous wings twice before dipping its head to aim straight at the earth below. It plummeted, quickly building to an impossibly fast speed. The scenery was still beautiful – fields, a river, trees – but the colours, Jack noticed, were all off. Trees were orange, the rivers red, the fields blue.

Jack flung his arms around the bird's neck,

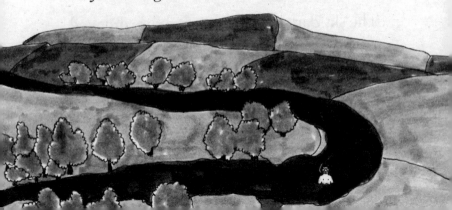

Cally threw her arms around Jack's waist, and they both clung on for dear life. The duck paid them no attention; its beak pointed straight down as it sliced through the air towards the ground.

Closer and closer came the ground, tighter Jack hugged the duck, tighter Cally hugged Jack, the wind tearing at their faces and hair, whipping and blasting.

And as the hard, blue ground rushed to meet them, the duck swung its huge head around and looked at Jack with dark, cold eyes. Its mouth broke into a mirthless grin, revealing two gleaming rows of perfect white teeth.

The duck winked once, opened its huge mouth wide and engulfed its own body, Jack and Cally and all. When the two rows of gleaming teeth slammed shut around them, all went dark.

"Where are we?" asked Jack. "It doesn't look like the inside of a duck. And where's the key gone?"

"I don't know," Cally said. "But we have our fingers and toes back."

She was right. Jack wiggled his fingers.

He lifted his bottom off the ground and dropped it down again.

Nothing.

"Yup," said Cally, clapping her hands together. They remained quiet.

"What about flying?"

"Don't know," said Cally. "Let's not find out. Not yet. I like the idea that it's still a possibility."

They looked around. A circular room. To their right a staircase wound up following the curve of the wall, spiralling up and up for as far

as they could see. Looking straight above them, this room too seemed to have no ceiling. The walls and the staircase disappeared out of sight eventually into a dazzling, blinding white light.

To their left began another staircase, again clinging to the line of the wall, but dropping round and down and out of sight into gradually thickening darkness.

"We have a choice here. Do we go up or down?" asked Cally.

"These stairs don't seem to lead anywhere."

"They *do* lead somewhere," said Cally. "That

one leads up, that one leads down. Come on, aren't you curious?"

Jack flattened himself against the wall.

Looking down into the chasm below made him feel dizzy, so he concentrated on the wall opposite.

"So, let's think," said Cally. "Up to the light or down to the dark? Light is 'good' normally, isn't it? **Light 'good', darkness 'bad'.** And up is normally a good thing: moving up, things are looking up. Heaven is up, isn't it? Hell is down. Your heart sinks and it's bad; your heart soars and that's good. People try to get to the top of their class, top of the league, top of their careers. But you might hit rock bottom, or you might break down."

"So..." said Jack. He needed to get off this platform.

"Well, I want to go up," said Cally. "Up feels safer, up feels more obvious. Think about it. Down is *feeling down in the dumps*. We can see where we're going if we go up."

"Down looks scary," said Jack. He began to smile. "I'm a little frightened by down."

"Why are you smiling?" Cally asked.

"When I think of going down into that darkness," Jack said, eyes shining, "it feels dangerous and it makes me feel a little sick. **And I think we need to do it.** Does that sound odd?"

"Not at all," she said. "I get it."

Jack wasn't entirely sure that he got it, but he felt elated by the risk.

"Come on."

Jack led the way and Cally followed. The walls were featureless, white and smooth. The staircase was only wide enough for them to walk in single file.

"I've been thinking," Cally said suddenly, "and I'm going to tell you how I got here. Or at least what happened just before I came here."

"OK."

"It's embarrassing," said Cally quietly.

"Try me," insisted Jack.

Cally sighed heavily.

"My grandma died and she–" Cally stopped and so did Jack. He turned to look at her.

"Keep going," Cally said. "I'm coming. Don't look at me."

They both set off. Gathering herself, Cally tried again.

"We're from an Irish family and there's this thing called a wake, where they have the body in the coffin in the house on the night before the funeral. Everybody comes to the house and some people get drunk and the dead body is just sitting there in a coffin with the lid off. You can walk up to it and look at it."

"Oh my god," said Jack, wide-eyed.

"That's not the embarrassing bit."

"Oh."

"I loved my gran," she said. "She sort of brought me up. My mum and dad got divorced when I was little and Dad had another family. And Mum was too ill and sad most of the time to take care of me. So Gran did."

"Oh."

"Whatever. You're just getting the main details here, I'm no good at telling stories. She wasn't perfect. She got angry with me sometimes, really shouted at me. But I guess I'd be annoyed if I had to spend my last few years looking after a kid because there was no one else to do it. Sometimes I hated her.

"But then she died. And that made my mum even more sad, and my dad wasn't much help because I didn't know him very well by then. His new wife didn't like me much. It was all horrible.

"It made me so angry. Her dying. **I was angry all the time. I still am.** I threw a pencil at my teacher, Miss Bolitho, who's actually really nice. She sent me to the head, who was kind to me. **That made me even more angry.**"

They continued down the staircase in silence for a moment.

"So anyway, it's the wake and Gran's dead in her coffin, in her front room, which was always a weird room that I hated. It was cold and we never used it. It had a spooky feeling.

"Loads of people came to the wake. Some family I didn't really know. My dad and his new wife and Mum in a state and some neighbours. I tried to go to bed but couldn't sleep because everyone was making so much noise. If Gran had still been there, she would have told everyone to go home. But she was dead so no one told them to go home. I couldn't do it because they wouldn't have listened to me even though it was my home – although it didn't feel like it any more. I wasn't sure where I would be going next. I came downstairs and I saw Mum sitting there, crying. She hadn't asked me how I was the whole time. **And something ... snapped.**

"I shouted at her that she was selfish and that I hated her and that she should stop trying to be the centre of attention when she and Gran didn't even like each other, which wasn't even true – I was just being horrible. Dad came out to see what was happening. I went into my room and I slammed my door, but Mum and Dad followed me in. There's no lock on that door so I couldn't stop them. So I ran downstairs. There was someone in the bathroom so I couldn't go in there. And there were people in the kitchen and the living room. People in every room. The only room with nobody in it was the dining room, which makes sense because who wants to drink and chat and eat crisps next to a dead body? So I ran in there and I slammed the door and I locked it and I just sat there staring at her. **At my dead gran.**

"I was so angry I could hardly breathe and suddenly I was crying so hard I thought I was going to choke. **It was scary. You better not tell anyone this.**"

Cally paused. Jack told himself to say nothing. To wait for her.

"She didn't look like herself," continued Cally eventually. "I can't explain it. People say that the dead are asleep but she didn't look asleep."

She stopped talking. For a few moments there was only the sound of their feet walking down the stairs.

"Anyway," Cally continued. "I could hear them all calling my name outside the door but I just sat there looking at Gran and I started to wonder what she felt like."

Jack flinched. He was worried about where this was going. "Go on."

"So, yeah," she said, "I touched her. I touched her face."

"Really?" Jack's mouth was so dry the word was barely audible.

"It gets worse."

"OK, I'm sorry. What did she feel like?"

"Cold. Really cold."

Another pause.

"So my finger is on her cheek and I'm thinking, this is my gran and she's dead. She was always there for me, even when she was grouchy. My dad wasn't. My mum wasn't because she wasn't well. But Gran was there for me even though we sometimes wanted to kill each other. And my finger was on her cheek. I just started to put a bit of pressure on it. I started to push. Just a little. A tiny amount. **And I'm in a sort of trance and all the sounds from the party start to fade away and all I'm focused on is this one bit of my gran's face and my finger on it and then someone shouts or laughs really loudly from the kitchen and I sort of come to and** see what I'm doing, that I've got my finger on my gran's face, and the shock and sudden realization makes me sort of spasm and my whole body twitches and my arms shoot up into the air and one of my knees comes up and slams into the bottom of the coffin, which is on a couple of stands, and I hurt my knee and I've kicked one of the stands which was holding up the head end and the whole thing, the coffin, my gran, everything starts to slide backwards towards the floor, so I reach out and try to grab it to stop it falling and I'm clinging on to both sides trying to keep it from falling over but it's too heavy for me to stop it and it slowly slides to the floor and I slide with it because I'm gripping both sides and as it falls, I fall too, and I fall into the coffin."

A silence.

"You fell into the coffin?" asked Jack slowly.

"Yeah. But I didn't land on her. I didn't touch her. Everything went dark. I landed in that room you found me in."

"No way."

"Don't act like that's so weird! You did a bungee jump and went right through the ground. Anyway, now you know. That's how I ended up here."

Jack didn't know what to say. Then he thought of his own mum.

"Sometimes you just aren't going to feel better," he found himself saying. Cally didn't reply.

"My dad never talked about it," he went on. "He tried to pretend it wasn't happening. I just wanted him to say, **"I feel it too. This is death. This is grief. This is happening. I feel it too."**

They walked in silence for a moment.

"Do you think that's why we're in here together?" asked Jack.

"Maybe. Who knows? You didn't throw any

pencils at anyone or slam doors though."

"No. I wish I could have. I just went all quiet. It was like I was locked inside my head and couldn't get out. I don't have the guts to shout and scream. But I was screaming inside. No one heard me."

"Well, I'm listening," said Cally.

"Yeah. If we can drink gorilla spit and survive, I reckon we can handle this," he grinned.

"Wish I'd drunk the tiger wee." Cally smiled. "And that's not something I ever thought I'd say!"

"Can you imagine what a nightmare this place would have been on our own?"

"I'd still be staring at those spiders," Cally shivered.

"I'd be smashed on the rocks!"

Jack wanted to tell Cally how glad he was

that she was there, how much he liked her, but he couldn't get himself to say the words out loud. He thought she might know anyway. He hoped she did.

So instead he said, "I don't know if I would have wanted my mum in her coffin in our dining room."

"Yeah. You really realize they are properly dead."

"That's the bit I don't think I want to know. Yet."

Cally stopped walking.

"Look! Jack!"

In the wall was a small door with a sign on it. The sign read:

"Come on," suggested Cally.

"No!" Jack said. **"Wanda said there were no**

shortcuts, remember?"

"Well, she was wrong. There *is* a shortcut. Right there. Look, your mum died, my gran died, all very sad and everything, but we've talked about it enough. I want to go home."

She put her hand on the door.

"You don't have to come with me, but it would be nice if you did."

"We can't split up!" protested Jack. "Wanda said we had to stick together!"

"See you later, Jack," said Cally and she pushed open the little door and squeezed through it.

Jack set his foot in the door to stop it closing and poked his head through. There was another set of stairs on the other side of the door and Cally was already heading down them.

"Cally!"

"It's been great," she called back.

Jack hesitated. **"Cally!"** he called again. No answer. Wanda had told them to avoid shortcuts. But she had also told them to stick together. With a sigh, he too pushed his way through the little door marked:  and raced down the stairs after her.

It didn't take him long to find Cally. She was standing on the staircase looking at another sign. This one said:

"We have one of those signs in the road outside our school," said Jack. "It means to be careful because there are kids around. Do you think there's a school down here?"

"I hope not," said Cally, "that would be rubbish."

"I think we should go back," said Jack.

"No way," said Cally. "Things are happening here. Those other stairs were taking for ever."

Jack walked down a little further, peering expectantly into the murkiness.

He could make out some shapes on the stairs. There was definitely something there. Four or five small figures moving gently, sluggishly down the stairs.

Jack called out,

"Hello!"

The shapes stopped moving and slowly turned to look up.

Jack and Cally rounded the final sweep of

the staircase. They could see the figures more clearly now. They were indeed short but very wide, as wide as two adults standing shoulder to shoulder. They rocked from side to side in an exaggerated fashion as they moved down the stairs. Hoods were pulled up over their heads, and each had a pair of huge eyes, which blinked languidly.

"Hello!" repeated Jack. **"I'm Jack and this is Cally. Who are you?"**

The figures stood and stared. Jack could see that they were wearing dark brown robes, which reminded him of monks' habits. The robes trailed on the ground behind them.

"Is this the way out?" Cally asked. Silence. "Can you at least tell us who you are?"

"We..." said the one nearest to Jack, its long eyelashes sweeping down and up over

its huge eyes, " ... **are** ..."

Those are insanely big eyes, thought Jack, two or three times bigger than normal.

" ... **the** ..."

Perhaps, thought Jack, they need those huge eyes because they live down here where it's so gloomy and dark all the time.

"... **the** ... **Slow** ... **Children**."

Jack and Cally waited for the child to say something else.

After a moment the Slow Children turned and began to walk down the stairs.

"Let's see where they are going," whispered Jack. "They have to be going somewhere."

Jack and Cally followed the hooded group. They walked incredibly slowly, rocking from side to side as they dropped down each step.

"Slow Children!?" hissed Cally into Jack's

ear. "They're not kidding."

"Excuse me," ventured Jack. "Could we squeeze past? We're in kind of a hurry."

The children stopped, stared at him, then turned and continued on their way.

"Please," said Cally impatiently.

Again the Slow Children came to a halt, shuffled around, stared at Jack and Cally, blinking.

"We just want to get past. Thank you!" said Jack cheerfully. He began to squeeze past the children.

"No," said one of the children. It took a step forward. **"No."**

The child may have been short but it possessed incredible strength, and Jack found himself pushed back against the white wall.

"Hey!" he said, half-laughing. "What are

you doing?"

"No," said the child. **"No."**

The other Slow Children had noticed what was happening. They stopped, turned around and came back up the steps to join their friend.

"No," they all began to say quietly but forcefully. **"No."**

Crowding around Jack, they too began to flatten him on to the wall with considerable force.

Behind them he could see Cally shouting, trying to get to Jack, to pull the Slow Children away, but to no avail. He began to struggle for breath. Jack couldn't hear what she was saying. All he could hear was the small, quiet, insistent **"No"** from the Slow Children, their big eyes staring sadly at him and showing no sign of effort as they crushed him against the wall.

"No."

The edges of his vision began to close in.

"No," they said. **"No."**

"BEDTIME! NOW!!!!"

From somewhere further down the staircase came a booming female voice, and the effect on the Slow Children was immediate. They released Jack, turned calmly and began to walk down the stairs.

Jack slid down the wall and Cally rushed to him.

"Are you OK?" asked Cally. Jack couldn't speak.

"HAVE YOU BRUSHED YOUR TEETH?" screamed the voice.

"Yes," said the Slow Children.

"HAVE YOU REALLY??" came the voice.

There was a pause.

"No," said the Slow Children, chastened.

"THEN DO IT NOW! BRUSH YOUR TEETH," thundered the instruction.

"AND GO TO THE TOILET BEFORE YOU GO TO BED. MAKE SURE YOU WASH YOUR HANDS AFTER YOU GO! I'M LOOKING AT YOU, DENNIS."

"Look!" said Cally to Jack, pointing down through the handrail. "We've reached the bottom!"

Once Jack was able to stand, they walked down to the bottom of the staircase.

The Slow Children were gone and there was no sign of the owner of the booming female voice.

The stairway opened out into a large basement, circular and dark. On the wall were hung framed posters, dozens of them.

Each poster showed happy-looking children or teenagers and each one had a saying printed on it.

"ANYONE CAN BE COOL ... BUT BEING AWESOME TAKES PRACTICE."

"AN APPLE A DAY KEEPS THE DOCTOR AWAY ... IF YOU THROW IT AT THEIR HEAD HARD ENOUGH!"

"Hee hee! That's my favourite!" said a voice behind them, making them jump.

It was the voice they'd heard shouting earlier, although the tone was now gentle. They turned to see a small hooded figure standing there. She was slightly bigger than the Slow Children but similar

AN APPLE A DAY
KEEPS THE DOCTOR AWAY

...IF YOU THROW IT AT
THEIR HEAD HARD ENOUGH!

looking – almost as wide as she was tall, with huge eyes.

"You expect it to say … **KEEPS THE DOCTOR AWAY** and stop there but it doesn't! It says … **IF YOU THROW IT AT THEIR HEAD HARD ENOUGH!** Which is not what you were expecting the second half of that sentence to be! That's why it's funny because you expect one thing but get something different. It's surprising."

Jack thought that her voice was very smooth. Calming. The kind of voice you'd want to listen to if you had trouble sleeping and you wanted someone to read you a relaxing bedtime story. No one had read him a bedtime story in a very long time.

"Although we wouldn't throw an apple at anyone's head in real life!" she continued, smiling. "Of course not. That's just a joke. There is a difference between a joke and real life. In real life you should treat people with respect. **In real life there are rules.**"

Jack looked to Cally to see if she was going to respond to the woman, but Cally just narrowed her eyes and stared at her.

"Er ... yes," said Jack. **"Respect is important."**

The woman smiled again. Jack noticed that her teeth were shorter than you'd expect in an adult. They looked like baby teeth. Her mouth, like her face and her body, was very wide and she seemed to have way more teeth than a mouth would normally contain.

"We should introduce ourselves," announced the woman, "so that we know who we are and what we are dealing with. **My name is Horatia von Spurkle.**"

"Oh hello, Horatia," said Jack. "I'm—"

"Ms von Spurkle. Call me 'Ms von Spurkle'," said Ms von Spurkle sharply.

"Oh, sorry. Hello, Ms Von Spurkle," said Jack. "Pleased to meet you. I'm Jack and this is—"

"Is this about what happened on the

stairs?" asked Cally. "We were only trying to get past."

"We will get to that presently," said Ms von Spurkle. **"Names first please."**

Cally narrowed her eyes. Jack did not like the way this was going. He could tell Cally and Ms von Spurkle were gearing up for a fight and that wouldn't help at all.

"I'm Jack," he repeated. "And this is—"

"Gertie," said Cally. She smiled sweetly. "I'm Gertie. **Gertie von Ham Press.** Pleased to meet you. Tell Ms von Spurkle your full name, Jack," said Gertie/Cally. "Oh, he's shy. **He's Jack Quail Zebedee Wigbert Doo Ron Ron Toilet Duck the Third.** But you can call him Terry. **Terry von Vonvon. Lord Terence von Trap de Vonvon."**

Jack thought he could see a door to his left but it was dark down there so he couldn't be sure.

"Anyway Ms von Spurkle, you wanted to talk to us about rules. . .?" asked Cally.

"I would," began Ms von Spurkle. She looked angry, thought Jack, although she was still smiling.

"Actually, hang on," said Cally, turning to Jack. "Would you rather be addressed as Lord Von de Vonvon or as your real name which is, of course, **Sir Leg Hair Trouser-Fire?**"

"Children!" shouted Ms von Spurkle in the booming voice they had heard earlier and from the gloom behind her emerged, rocking from side to side as they walked, about a dozen Slow Children. They fanned out in a long line either side of Ms von Spurkle. It took them quite some time to do so.

"Hi, guys," said Jack. **"What's up? Sorry**

about what happened on the stairs. No hard feelings, eh?"

"You must not push past anyone on the stairs," said Ms von Spurkle. "That is the rule. What is the rule?"

"Don't push past anyone on the stairs," intoned the Slow Children.

"Rules are there to be obeyed," said Ms von Spurkle.

"Obey," said the Slow Children.

"Well, we said we were sorry," said Cally.

"You broke the rules," said Ms von Spurkle. **"You must be punished."**

"Punished," echoed the children.

"What are you going to do?" asked Cally.

The Slow Children began to chomp their little teeth together in a rhythmic, co-ordinated beat.

It made quite a noise.

CHOMP.

The sound of all those short teeth smashing into each other.

CHOMP.

They opened their mouths slowly until they were as wide as it was possible for them to be then. . .

CHOMP.

It was intimidating.

CHOMP.

"You are going to be punished. Rules are rules. And you broke them."

CHOMP.

"We're going to eat you."

CHOMP.

"Sorry, what?" said Jack.

CHOMP.

The Slow Children began walking towards Jack and Cally, rocking sideways as they went.

CHOMP.

As they did so, Ms von Spurkle clapped her hands and the staircase behind her started to lift in the air, up and out of reach.

CHOMP.

Instinctively Jack and Cally moved closer to each other as they backed away from the Slow Children, who were advancing slowly but steadily in a line towards them. Behind them were only solid walls.

CHOMP.

The only way out now seemed to be past the Slow Children and Ms von Spurkle.

But the Slow Children were blocking the way, and after the incident on the staircase Jack was only too aware just how strong they were.

CHOMP.

"You took the shortcut," said Ms von

Spurkle. "You weren't prepared to see the Rooms through. And now you belong to me."

CHOMP.

Cally leaned into Jack's ear and whispered, "We're making this too easy for them, sticking together like this. Let's split up and on my signal run through the middle. OK?"

Jack had gone as white as a sheet but he managed to nod. He and Cally moved apart from each other as the children continued their slow approach.

CHOMP.

The Slow Children split into two groups. Half swung in Jack's direction, half turned towards Cally.

Ms von Spurkle, who had been in the middle of the line, joined the children advancing on Cally. A gap opened up in the middle. Jack gasped as his back hit the wall. *Come on, Cally,* he thought. *It's now or never.*

CHOMP.

"Now!" shouted both Cally and Jack at exactly the same time, and they hurled themselves towards the gap that had opened up between the two lines of children.

"NO!!!!" screamed Ms von Spurkle in fury. **"STOP THEM!"**

Jack slipped between the outstretched arms of the children and Ms von Spurkle but Cally, immediately behind him, wasn't so lucky.

Ms von Spurkle placed a meaty hand on Cally's arm and yanked her backwards with tremendous force. Cally's feet left the ground and she shrieked in surprise as she flew through the air, landing on the ground in a crumpled heap.

The rest of the children waddled together so that they now formed a solid line again with Jack on one side of it and Cally on the other.

"Go!" shouted Cally. **"Just go! Get help!"**

Jack stood rooted to the spot. His way was clear. But he couldn't abandon Cally. He couldn't leave her here alone.

"Go or they'll get us both!" Cally shouted at him. **"Please."**

Jack looked at his escape route and then he looked back to Cally. He didn't want to be eaten by these creatures. And this had all been Cally's fault. She had insisted on the shortcut. She had broken the rules.

He made a decision.

"I'm going, Cally!" he yelled. **"I'm sorry. I'm really sorry. But there's no point in us both dying."**

And Jack turned and ran away.

Cally sat on the floor and stared up at Ms von Spurkle.

"You know you can leave whenever you like," said Ms von Spurkle quietly. **"You can be free right now if you want. You just need to tell me that you never cared for her. That's what the shortcut is. You know that, don't you?"**

"What? Who?"

"You know who. Your grandmother."

"I'm not afraid of you," said Cally defiantly, tears welling in her eyes. **"I am not afraid."**

"You took the shortcut *because* you are afraid. You couldn't deal with this process any longer. Tell me that you didn't really care for her. It's the only thing keeping you here. Give up on her and you'll be free to go. You wanted a shortcut, this is it."

Cally swallowed. "It wouldn't be true. I'd be betraying her."

"She's dead. She's gone. She'll never know. Think of all the times you argued. How strict she was with you. She didn't want to look after you, did she? She was stuck with you. And you hated her for that. You hate her for leaving you. Say it, Cally."

The line of children swayed from side to side. Cally eyed them fearfully.

"Why didn't you tell Jack this?"

"He is on a different path. But you . . . you're halfway there already. Just say it."

Cally looked at Horatia and then at the Slow Children rocking from side to side, their rows of bared teeth. Her mind was foggy. She couldn't think straight. And she *was* angry with her gran. She had been horrible at times.

"Hurry up," said Horatia sharply. **"We're not going to wait all day."**

Cally took a deep breath. She opened her mouth to speak, and—

From her right came a loud, primal scream and Cally turned to see Jack throwing himself at the end Slow Child. For a moment the Slow Child wobbled on one leg, a look of surprise on her face, mouth and eyes wide open in astonishment, arms flailing.

It was like trying to tip over a small car. If the weight pivoted back towards Jack, he'd be crushed. Jack shoved with every ounce of his strength. Cally held her breath.

But then, languidly, almost gracefully, the child began to fall. Over the Slow Child went into the Slow Child next to her, who swayed and wobbled and went over too. And he into the next one. And she into the next one. All the way down the line. A chain reaction, like a line of dominoes, until they were all sprawled helplessly on their backs, their short limbs thrashing about.

Ms von Spurkle lunged at Cally, grabbing a handful of her jacket.

"Not so fast, you horrible thug," she snarled into Cally's ear. **"You're all mine."**

Cally spun on the spot and, throwing her arms behind her, slipped out of the jacket, freeing herself. In one big leap she hurdled the writhing Slow Children lying on the floor and joined Jack.

"You'll never catch us," said Cally triumphantly to Ms von Spurkle. **"And I'd never have betrayed my gran. Never."**

"Easy to say now," she snarled. **"And I wouldn't be so sure that we can't catch you. Come on, kids."**

In a flash the Slow Children sprang to their feet and, flinging their mouths open wide, they ran, fast, at Cally and Jack, who turned and fled down the corridor.

Jack and Cally were both good runners but so were the Slow Children, who were

quickly gaining on them. Jack didn't dare turn around to look but it felt like they were already almost close enough to touch him.

"How come they got so fast?" he gasped.

The leading Slow Child reached out a hand to grab him, but Jack saw it out of the corner of his eye and swerved slightly, throwing the Slow Child off balance as he lunged for Jack and into the path of the child next to him. The children tripped each other up and both went down, shrieking as they did so.

The Slow Child immediately behind them stumbled too, falling head over heels, emitting a high-pitched piercing scream as he fell.

Almost instantly all three were back on their feet and after Jack and Cally again, heads flung back, mouths open wide.

The corridor was becoming narrower.

What happens if we hit a dead end? thought Jack.

Cally spotted a squat wooden stool ahead on Jack's side of the passageway.

"Jack!" she said, pointing at it.

He knew what she was getting at. As they passed the stool Jack swooped and picked it up. In one motion he turned and threw it at the pack of Slow Children behind them. The chair sailed through the air towards the leading child, who watched it arc towards her without making any effort to avoid it. Jack watched, horrified. He'd wanted to slow the child down, not hit her.

The running child threw her mouth open wider and snapped at the stool, biting down hard, splintering it into hundreds of small pieces and, without breaking stride, kept

charging at Jack,

small arms and legs pumping like pistons.

"Wow!" was all Jack could say.

Jack and Cally strained every muscle to run as fast as they could but there was no doubt that the Slow Children were still gaining on them.

"Look!" shouted Cally, pointing ahead.

A wall directly ahead. Jack's worst fears were realized: a dead end!

But as they got closer, they saw there were corridors running off on either side: one to the left and one to the right.

"Which way?" panted Cally.

"Pretend to go left then go right. On my signal," gasped Jack.

Little arms were reaching out to grab them, one even got a brief hold of Cally before she swatted it away.

"Come on!" urged Jack, and Cally gritted her teeth and re-doubled her effort.

"Now!" shouted Jack, and both he and Cally darted to the left as if to take that passage and almost immediately swerved to the right.

It worked! The Slow Children may have been fast but they were not nimble, and Jack and Cally's sudden change in direction caused the front two to trip and fall, skidding and twisting to the ground, their backs hammering into the wall with tremendous force.

One after the other the Slow Children, unable to stop in time, stumbled and fell, and as Jack and Cally darted down the corridor they could hear the children slamming with dull thuds into the brick wall.

"Yes!" screamed Jack. **"YES!"**

Running through an arch, Jack and Cally

emerged into a small courtyard. After the gloomy darkness they squinted in the bright daylight.

Behind them they could hear the moans of the Slow Children as they struggled to their feet.

In front of them was a brick wall roughly twice their height. There was no door, no window, no gate. No way out.

"**Quick**," said Jack, "I'll give you a leg up."

"What about you?"

"You can pull me up. Hurry."

Jack stood with his back to the wall and cupped his hands on one knee. Cally placed her right foot on it and reached up for the top of the wall. Jack shook with the effort. Cally managed to get an elbow on to the top of the wall. Swinging her leg up and over, she pivoted her body around until she sat on the top of the wall, one leg dangling down either side.

She reached down.

"Come on, jump and I'll pull you up."

But Jack was frozen to the spot, looking back the way they came.

She followed his gaze. Striding towards him, calmly, was Horatia von Spurkle.

"JACK!" shouted Cally. "Come on!"

She took off a shoe and threw it, hitting Jack on the shoulder. Startled, he looked up at her.

"Move!" she barked.

Jack came out of his reverie, ran a few paces away from the wall, turned, sprinted back towards it, and with every ounce of effort he could muster he jumped as high as he could, reaching, straining for the top of the wall. Cally lunged for him but missed.

"Take a bigger run up," urged Cally.

With a yell of triumph Horatia burst out of the corridor and into the courtyard, followed by the children. Jack tensed, but to his surprise, Horatia and the Slow Children had stopped running and were crying out in pain, their hands clutched over their eyes.

"The light! They're not used to it. They're blinded!" said Jack.

"Not for long though," said Cally. "They'll adjust. We have to hurry."

Jack looked behind him. Cally was right. Ms von Spurkle was already walking towards him, shielding her eyes and groping blindly with one hand.

"Take off your other shoe," hissed Jack to Cally, "and when I say, drop it to the floor."

"What? Why?"

"Just do it!" insisted Jack.

"I'm here, Horatia," he said loudly and defiantly, moving a couple of steps further along the wall. **"But I'm stronger than you. You'll never beat me."**

Horatia chuckled, pivoting towards the sound of Jack's voice.

"Is that so?" she said as she closed in on him.

"It is!" said Jack. "I – I learn judo."

"Judo!" boomed Horatia. **"Oh well, then I'm no match for you then. Judo!"**

266

She roared with laughter.

"You'll see," said Jack, back flat against the wall.

Above, Cally looked on helplessly, shoe in hand.

Jack looked up and mouthed, **"Now!"** to Cally, who dropped the shoe.

As it hit the ground, Horatia spun round, reaching down towards the sound.

Jack didn't hesitate. He raced at Ms von Spurkle and jumped on to her back.

As Horatia felt his weight on her, she stood up, her powerful legs unwittingly lifting Jack to exactly where he wanted to be. Jack leaped for the top of the wall, pulled himself up in one deft movement, and he and Cally quickly lowered themselves down the other side.

They dropped to the ground and stood

there, stunned, hardly able to believe that they were now free.

From the other side of the wall came a pitiful and eerie howling. Jack and Cally looked around. They appeared to be in some sort of park, in the middle of which was one small but perfectly formed hill. At the top of the hill stood two people.

"Look!" said Jack. **"It's Wanda and Gary!"**

Jack and Cally walked to the top of the hill. It was a gloriously sunny day, not a cloud in the sky, and they enjoyed the warm sun on their skin after so much time inside.

"Did we leave the Rooms?" asked Jack.

"I'm not sure," Cally said.

Wanda looked extraordinary. Her hair was tied up using pink and orange balloons, the kind used by people who make balloon animals. Over her mouth was a surgical mask which had a massive mouth painted on it, much bigger than Wanda's actual mouth and slightly off-centre. Her jacket had two huge lapels made of stiff brown leather extending wider than her body, there was a chain mail belt around her torso, a cape with a picture of two llamas eating waffles over the words **"WAFFLE HOUSE"**, a pink tutu, bloomers, and the lower part of her legs were wrapped in bandages that looked like they had been drawn all over by an infant with a crayon. On her feet were a pair of slippers that looked like yeti's feet, complete with claws and straggly grey fur.

In one hand she was holding a bouquet, in the other a duck on a lead. The duck stood quietly by her side and was also wearing a cape, with the words "I hate waffles" written on it.

Next to her was Gary wearing jeans, trainers and a T-shirt that said: **"I'D RATHER BE EATING BISCUITS"**.

"Well, hello!" cooed Wanda. **"You are just in time! We're getting married!"**

"You and Gary?" asked Cally. She didn't want to be rude, but she couldn't see those two together at all.

"No, don't be silly," laughed Wanda. "I think the only thing Gary would consider marrying would be a fig roll."

"Don't like fig rolls," said Gary sulkily.

"You're marrying a duck?" was all Jack could manage.

"I am," Wanda purred. "He's called William of Orange. Say hello!"

"Hello, William," said Jack self-consciously.

"I was talking to the duck," said Wanda tartly.

They looked down at William of Orange expectantly but he said nothing.

"How are you two doing?" asked Wanda.

"We're OK now," said Cally. "Horatia von Spurkle was . . . a bit of a challenge."

"Oh dear, you took the shortcut? That's disappointing."

"Do we have to go back into the Rooms and finish properly?" asked Jack anxiously.

Wanda looked surprised. **"No! You were basically finished anyway. The shortcut takes longer than the regular route. That's the whole point. That's why I said, 'Don't take the shortcut.'"**

Jack looked at Cally and smiled. She shrugged.

"Anyway, you're done!" exclaimed Wanda. **"This is goodbye."**

"Really?" Jack could scarcely believe her. **"We can go?"**

"Remember what I said when we first met? 'The Rooms are here for you and you are here for the Rooms. To get to where you need to be, you will have to journey through them.' Shall I do the song?"

"NO!" said Jack quickly. "No, thank you."

"Whevs," Wanda said with dignity. "Listen,

there will be lots of other rooms, but you know what to do now. Deal with one room at a time. Keeping looking for the answer. Stick at it. And you know now that you can do it."

"And most importantly. . .?" asked Gary.

"Don't shove too many biscuits in your gob at once?" said Cally.

"Nearly. It's 'Sometimes there are no biscuits, so get them when you can'."

"Oh, right."

"You need to get back, don't you?" asked Wanda. "You have lives to lead."

Neither Jack nor Cally moved.

"Hello?!" said Wanda, waving a hand in front of their faces. "Earth to Planet Duvet, do you read me?"

"I just can't believe it's over," said Jack.

"I mean, it's not *completely* over," said

Wanda. "You're going back to your real lives. There will be stuff going on, yeah? There always is."

Cally nodded.

"But this bit? Done. So, say your goodbyes, you two."

"Right, yes," said Jack, suddenly shy.

He and Cally turned to each other.

"Thanks, mate," she said simply. **"Good luck."**

Jack smiled back.

"You too."

There was an awkward pause.

"So what happens now?" asked Jack.

"Watch," Wanda beamed. **"This is good, you'll like this."**

The clear blue sky began to bruise, gently flushing with blues and reds and yellows.

Washes of the lightest greens and oranges and pinks pulsed and flickered. Shapes emerged, indistinguishable, then melted away. Above, bands of cerulean and azure and aquamarine throbbed, lighter areas congealing into soft bundles of creamy clouds which skidded low and fast.

Below their feet, umber and chocolate browns churned and rippled, streaked with greens of emerald and olive and jade. The colours danced and flickered, mingled and splintered. A sudden blinding flash and Jack felt himself flicked upside down by an unseen force and, feet first, he flew at an incredible speed upwards, aware of Cally by his side for a fleeting moment. The sky convulsed again and darkened instantly, he felt a rush of cool air, and became aware of the smell of burgers and petrol, the sound of distant screams and music, bright lights below him, stars above, as he arced gracefully into the night sky, his ankles attached to a long elastic rope, the rope attached to a crane, the fairground far below.

Once he'd stopped bouncing up and down, the crane gently lowered him to the ground. Tilly and Bobby gave him a thumbs up and, he was sure, a slight wink.

Jack undid the harness around his legs and scrambled up and away. He ran towards the fair without looking back.

Sliding along the passageway between the two rides, stepping gingerly over the thick electrical cables underfoot, he emerged from the darkness into the tumult of the fair in full swing.

Stepping into the light he almost collided with Niblet and Beano, who hurtled past him at breakneck speed.

Niblet was howling with laughter; Beano was shouting, **"I'll kill you for that!"**

Jack fought his way through the crowds and was surprised and delighted to see his father standing there, still flicking through his phone.

"Dad," said Jack breathlessly.

"That was quick," said his father. "Now what? Home?"

"No," said Jack, relieved and bewildered that his father hadn't noticed that he'd been gone for ages. "Let's do something exciting. What about the Sky Scream?"

"Really?! Won't you hate it?"

"Maybe," said Jack, "but I won't know until I've tried it, will I?"

"Wow, all right, let's do it," said his dad. "Don't do it just for me though."

"I'm not," said Jack. **"Might be fun. What's the worst that can happen?"**

At that moment, Niblet barged through, still screaming with laughter, pursued by Beano.

"Hey, Beano!" shouted Jack.

Beano screeched to a halt as Niblet disappeared into the crowd.

"Oh. All right, Jack. You OK?"

"Yeah, I'm good. Would you do me a favour?"

"What's that?"

"Take a pic of me and my dad."

They walked back together in silence from the fair an hour later, past the Princess of Wales pub, across the bridge over the canal, left at the newsagents with the phone box outside.

I wonder, thought Jack as they drew close to home, *I wonder if I told him where I have been tonight, what has happened to me, whether he would believe me?* He thought how his father might react to being told Jack had had a conversation with a frog, and for a while had had toes for fingers.

The thought of trying to explain his adventure made Jack laugh out loud.

"What's funny?" asked his dad.

"Oh . . . just thinking about the Sky Scream," said Jack, smiling.

Turning into their road, the sound of a front door being flung open made them glance over. Jack could hear the clamour of people inside the house, a party of some sort. A woman came running out of the house crying out in surprise, a man followed close behind, stumbling slightly

as he came down the front steps. The couple rushed up to a smaller third person Jack hadn't noticed at first, standing in the shadows of the front garden. The three of them hugged, forming a tight little group, and Jack could hear them laugh. Then the smaller figure looked up and caught Jack's eye, her mouth opening in surprise. Cally.

She raised a hand and smiled at Jack as he walked by.

"One room," she called out. **"One room at a time!"**

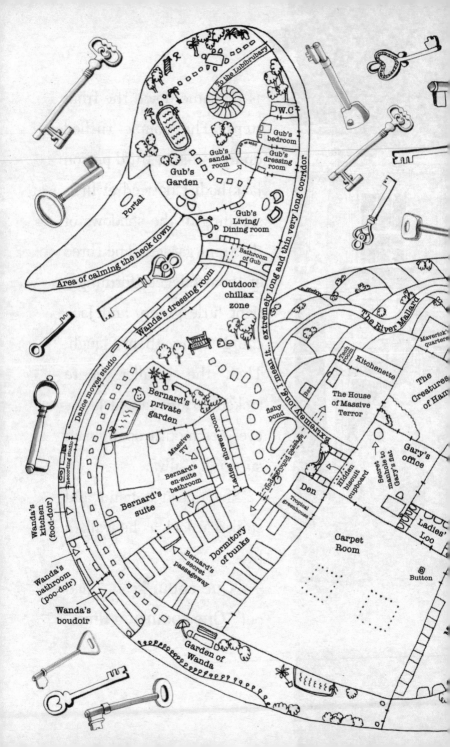

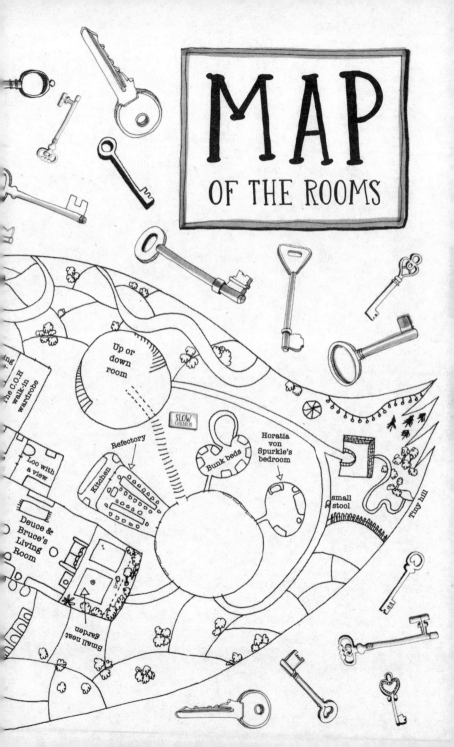

STEPHEN MANGAN is a Tony-nominated actor known for his roles in *Green Wing, I'm Alan Partridge* and *Episodes*. Stephen also voiced the title role in *Postman Pat: The Movie*. He was a member of the judging panel for the 2020 Costa Book of the Year prize.

🐦 @StephenMangan

ANITA MANGAN is a successful illustrator and designer who has worked on award-winning books for the Leon brand, Gizzi Erskine, Fearne Cotton, Ella's Kitchen, Comptoir Libanais and the bestselling *'Be a Unicorn, Sloth, Flamingo...'* series.

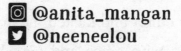

🅾 @anita_mangan
🐦 @neeneelou

ACKNOWLEDGEMENTS

Firstly, my wonderful sister, Anita, who has always been gifted as an artist in contrast to my total lack of ability. In this book she takes the opportunity to further rub my talentless nose in it. If any of you ever find yourselves writing a book that requires illustrations, my recommendation is to have a sister who can creatively knock it out of the park and make the process full of joy at the same time.

Thanks to Fiz Osborne at Scholastic for reading an interview Anita and I gave to the *Sunday Times* and spotting a potential book off in the distance. Lauren Fortune was my estimable editor and kicked me and this book into shape with grace and patience. Thanks too to everyone else at Scholastic who made me look better than I could have reasonably expected to and to Paul Stevens at Independent.

A special mention to Peter Nixon who was 'that' teacher at school for me, introducing me to the worlds of theatre and acting, films and film-making, books and reading – it's all his fault. He gave some insightful notes during the writing of this story.

And, finally, but most importantly, to my boys: Harry, Frank and Jack, and to Louise, who are my whole world and who push me to work harder to be funny by never laughing at any of my jokes. Except Jack – he laughs at them and now he has the main character in a book named after him so **THINK ON'T.**

THANKS FOR
JOINING US...

SEE YOU SOOOO

OOOOOOOOON!

AND
REMEMBER...

THE
ROOMS
ARE HERE
FOR YOU...

AND YOU ARE HERE FOR THE ROOMS